Nichol
1946.

MACMILLAN AND CO., Limited
LONDON · BOMBAY · CALCUTTA · MADRAS
MELBOURNE

THE MACMILLAN COMPANY
NEW YORK · BOSTON · CHICAGO
DALLAS · SAN FRANCISCO

THE MACMILLAN CO. OF CANADA, Ltd.
TORONTO

IN THE
LAND OF YOUTH

BY

JAMES STEPHENS

MACMILLAN AND CO., LIMITED
ST. MARTIN'S STREET, LONDON
1924

CHAPTER I

It was decided that the evening meal should
be eaten on the lawn before the palace. A
tent had been set under a tree and a fire was
built in front of it. Torches were tied to the
branches of the tree, and others were fixed to
stakes driven into the ground; so there was
plenty of light; and in the ring cast by these
flares there was great animation.

But beyond this circle, where the smoke
went drifting in grey billows, night was
already brooding, and minute by minute the
darkness became deep and deeper.

No stars were visible. There was no sky
to be seen. There was nothing for the eye
to rest on. And if a man had placed his hand
before his face he would not have been able
to see his hand.

Little by little the last loitering couples
were driven from dusk vistas to the centre

of the lawn; and little by little the merry talk became grave, and the loud voices were hushed. Soon there was no one moving outside the circle of light except servants who had to draw water from the well, or perform other outdoor duties.

Even these did not move abroad, for this was the month of Samhain,[1] and the one night of the year in which whoever has the will and the courage may go to Faery.[2]

The servants even did not stir without. They had accumulated all the water which could possibly be used that night. The storehouses, the piggeries, the sheep-cotes and hen-roosts had been closed for the night; and around each of these, and all around Cruachan Ai, and all about every hamlet in Ireland, incantations had been uttered, and magical circles drawn against the Masters of Magic.

While waiting for the meats to be brought, Ailill lay in the opening of the tent staring beyond the fire at that great blackness. Maeve was at the back of the tent sharing nuts that had been stewed in honey between

---

[1] Samhain: pronounced "Sow'in".
[2] Now All-Hallows Eve.

4

three royally clamorous children, and exchanging apples with Fergus mac Roy, and glances also which were meant for no other eye than his.   Other people also were stretched about the tent, chattering aimlessly and all impatient for their supper.

"The meal will be ready soon," said Maeve.   "It is late because of the games, but it will be ready very soon now."

Or she would detail his future to an impatient champion:

"There is roast meat and boiled, my dear. There is fish stewed in milk, and birds boiled with spices.   There are puddings of minced flesh and sweet bread.   There is white thin milk, and thick yellow milk.   There are many different kinds of broth.   There is wine from far countries, and mead, my love, made by myself from the honey gathered by my own bees in the flowers that grow about Cruachan.   And after that there is ale, and red-cheeked apples."

"It will be ready very soon, my darlings."

CHAPTER II

" I wonder would any man dare go abroad to-night," said Ailill, as he stared against the darkness. " I seem to hear already the brisk tread of the people of Dana moving out there beyond the light."

" I hear something," a companion averred.

" You hear the wind stirring in lazy branches," said a third.

" Was *that* the wind? "

" It was a ferret."

" Was it so? " Ailill queried. " If you will go to the hill where the outlaws were hanged yesterday, and if you will tie a withy round the foot of one of the hanging men, I will give you a present."

" I'll do that."

But in two minutes the man returned, saying that he heard things moving, and did not care to go farther.

" I thought you would come back, my pulse," said Ailill.

Two others ventured, and returned terrified.

" The night is dark, and there are demons

6

about," said Maeve, " no man would go out on the eve of Samhain, even for a prize."

Then Nera stepped forward.

" What prize are you offering, Majesty?"

" This gold-hilted sword," the King replied, looking at him mockingly.

" I will go," said Nera.

" Go, with my love," said the King, "but," as Nera stepped from the tent, " I shall expect you back in a minute, dear heart."

" I will come for my prize," said Nera.

He walked through the flare of the torches, and the company watched him go.

He came to the end of the lawn where the light began to fail, and, as he walked, he looked closely at what light was left.

Here the light was golden, and here it became grey, and here, a step farther, it became blue or purple, and here, but two paces beyond, it was no longer a colour; it was a blackness, an invisibility.

It would be wrong to say that the young man was not afraid. Given the night and the deed that he had undertaken, any man might have shown the fear which he kept hidden. But his will was set, and he knew

that, even if he could not go on, he would
not turn back; so he bent his mind inflexibly
on the hill before him, and on the swinging
figures which he had to meet.

The man whose mind is thus set is con-
scious of himself to that extent, but in other
and curious ways he has ceased to be quite his
own master, for while the mind is concen-
trated and engaged on one sole matter we are
blind and deaf to all others, and we may be
interfered with beyond our knowledge.

Nera turned to look over his shoulder, and,
when he saw the tent, now curiously distant
and precise, and the figures that moved un-
hurriedly about it, it was as though he were
peeping into or at another world.

Then he set out with long, strong paces
in the direction of the hill.   But he kept his
sword in his hand and his buckler on his arm.

CHAPTER III

HE knew his way to the hill.   Indeed, he had
been there on the previous day when these
malefactors were swung, and he remem-

bered that they had been a troublesome couple.

One of them had said:

" It is not often that notable miscreants are ended, and everybody has a right to look on wonders. There are not enough women present," he complained.

The other outlaw contented himself with a criticism of all that was done for him, and of the looks and qualities of his guard. When the rope had been fixed on his neck he yawned so widely that it was disarranged, and had to be settled again.

" Keep your yawns to yourself," said the captain of the guard, " and please to let my men do their duty."

" I'm sleepy," the outlaw objected.

" Even if you are," said the captain of the guard, " you need not hinder my men."

" One must be polite in company," said the outlaw, " so I'll do my best not to yawn until you have finished with me."

He did his best.

The other rogue remarked that he had become thirsty standing all that time.

" There is nothing here to drink," the captain returned.

9

" It doesn't matter," the rogue answered. " It just struck me, and I mentioned it."

Nera remembered these men, and he remembered in especial the face of the thirsty man — a long, hatchet-face, with a great nose on it, and a close-curling beard on the chin. He had seemed to be thinking deeply and discontentedly at the last moment, and had obviously dismissed what was happening about him for more private imaginings.

As he walked the face of this man appeared before him with such suddenness that he almost drove at it with his sword; but, recognising at the same instant that it was merely his imagination at play, he banished the phantom and went on.

Although he knew the way so well it was nevertheless not easy to keep to it in that darkness, and he paused a few times to reconstruct the path he had already come, and to calculate from it the direction in which he should continue.

He had not far to go.

Barely five minutes' march lay between the lawn of Royal Cruachan and the place towards which he was bent, and, given only a general direction, he could not miss the hill.

He passed through a bushy place which swished and crackled about his ears; came out on turf that sank and rose with its clear elastic noise; and then he came on the rising ground which told that the hill had begun.

He held the sword thrust in front of him as he trod upwards, not to ward off goblins, but so that he might feel if a tree was in his path or a boulder.

There were not many trees to be sure, but there were huge outcropping rocks carved to every kind of edge and knob and projection that one could think of, and if a man stumbled against one of these his skull could be broken, or his shin bone might get a crack that would leave him hopping for a month.

CHAPTER IV

HE came to the top of the hill, and found that, careful as he had been, he had yet moved somewhat from the direct path, and was some score of yards east of the point he aimed for.

Up here it was not so dark as it had been among the trees and boulders below. Or perhaps the fact that he was on an eminence tended to make him look upwards and catch such rays of light as there might be.

While walking below he had kept his eyes to the ground, following, although not seeing, his feet; and adding, thus, to the darkness that descended from the atmosphere the deeper blackness which arose from the ground. Or it might be that his eyes had become more accustomed to darkness, and, although he could not exactly see, he could, as it were, surmise; for he began to distinguish between the various darknesses that lay about him, and was aware of gradations among these dusks.

Here there was the black of ebony—it was a boulder.

Here was a sketchy incomplete blackness —it was a bush.

Beyond was not a blackness but a darkness, and that was space.

Beneath him there was a velvet gloom, and that was the ground.

And above there was a darkness, not to be described, but to be thought of, as a movement, and that was the sky.

He moved to the right searching for the one tree which grew on the hill, and, after a cautious exploration, he found it, and stood listening to the slow creakings which told that this was indeed his tree.

As he moved forward a foot tapped him gently on the mouth, and he leaped back with his sword uplifted, staring blindly, and listening with all his blood.

Then he smiled to himself, rattled the sword into its scabbard, and, putting his hand resolutely forward, he laid hold of that foot.

CHAPTER V

HE took the withy he had prepared out of his belt and began to fix it on the foot, but the thing was too elastic, and each time that he thought he had it right it sprang open.

From above his head, out of and into darkness, there came a hoarse and bubbling whisper, a rusty stammering that thudded his heart most out of his breast and his soul all but out of his body.

" You'll never tie it that way," said the

13.

voice. "Put a peg into it, decent man, or stick your brooch through it if you have no peg."

Nera almost let go the foot, but a savage obstinacy came on him, and he bit with his upper teeth on his lower lip until he nigh bit it in two.

"Very well," said he to the voice, "I'll stick my brooch in."

He did so, and the withy held.

"You are not dead?" said he to the man above him.

"Not out and out," the man replied.

"How does it happen that you are still alive?"

"It happened this way," replied that creaky and rusty tone; "when they were hanging me I was very thirsty, and ever since I have been too thirsty to die."

"It is a hard case," said Nera.

"Well," said he then, "I'll be moving, for I'm going to get a prize for what I did to-night to your foot."

"It was a good manly job," said the voice.

"It was," Nera admitted, "considering the kind of thing I had to do, and the sort of night in which I had to do it."

14

" But," said the voice above, " prove to me that you are really a courageous man."

" How would I prove that? " Nera asked.

" Take me down off this tree and carry me to some place where I can get a drink."

" You've been sentenced to be hanged," Nera replied, " and you've got to hang."

" That's all right," the voice answered, " I don't want to dodge Doom. You could bring me back after I got the drink, and you could hang me up again."

" I don't like the job," said Nera.

" I wouldn't like it myself," the voice replied, " but it would be a charitable act, and a valorous one."

" That is true," said Nera, " and I'll do what you ask."

" For," he continued, " there never was a man in the world before was asked to do the like; and there isn't a man in the world but myself would do it."

Nera then began to climb the tree.

squawk tumbling off the end of her tongue the way water tumbles off a ledge.

There were three buckets of water standing by the wall. Nera propped his man against the door, and held one of the buckets to his lips. He drank a bucket dry. Then he drank the other two buckets dry.

"That's not a bad drink," said Nera, "and if you're not satisfied 'tis because nothing will satisfy you. Come back to your torment, my soul."

He picked up the malefactor, hunched him on to his back, and went out of the house with him and back to the hill.

As he strung him up he asked:

"Do you feel any better now, my darling?"

"I feel splendid," said the outlaw. "I'll be dead in a jiffey."

Nera left him then, swinging easily and buoyantly, and he took the road back to Cruachan of the Dun Ramparts, for he was impatient to get his prize.

CHAPTER VII

" I HAVE been a good while away," said Nera to himself. " No man can say I was afraid, for I shouldn't have stayed out so long, and on the night of Samhain, if I had been afraid."

He thought also that it would be a fine thing to own a gold-hilted sword, and he wondered if the blade would be as good as the blade of his own weapon was; for, after all, it is not the hilt that is important in a sword.

Musing thus, he came in good time to Cruachan, and on the skirt of the lawn, just beyond the fringe of light, he halted.

There was far more light coming from the lawn than there had been when he went away.

Not only was the fire burning before the tent, the tent was burning; and behind it the vast mass of the palace was spouting flame at every window and vomiting fire from an hundred different parts of the roof.

With the raging uproar of flame there came a babel of other noises; yells of de-fiance, and roars of encouragement; torrents

19

of imprecations, and the dismal yapping of wounded men.

A man came bursting from that torment of noise and flame. He ran past Nera with his desperate eyes staring, and nothing in his hand but the splintered handle of a spear.

Nera recognised with a shock that the man had looked at him and had not seen him.

In a few minutes three or four others came flying in his direction, and they also darted past without a halt, without even the recognition of voice or eye.

When another man came, Nera thrust himself into his path, and, to his surprise and horror, the man ran through him.

Then Nera recognised that he was neither in the world nor out of the world. That he was between worlds—that he was in Faery.

He rushed into the circle of light to the tent. Outside it he saw the body of Ailill stretched on its back, one arm thrown over the face and the other lying along the ground with the hand still gripping a broken sword. Within the tent Maeve was lying with her head huddled into her knees, and a dark pool forming about her. Fergus was tumbled a pace beyond, and here and there other bodies lay in every aspect of abandonment and ignominy. Everywhere soldiers were running with red weapons and roaring mouths. He ran into one of these, and that man was solid as a rock.

" Join the work, comrade, join the work," the man shouted with a great laugh.

Nera said to himself: " This is a man of the Shí, and he takes me to be one of his host."

" Alas," he thought, " all my friends are dead, or they are flying on the desolate hills in that bleak, bitter darkness, and I am translated."

But the wild work was finished, and the victorious fairy troop was re-forming into its companies and regiments, and were beginning their march back to the Shí in the enchanted Hill of Cruachan.

CHAPTER VIII

NERA did not wish to go with them, and yet he could not conceive of anything else to do. He felt far more lost than even a lost dog can feel. Not alone had he lost his comrades, his world and all his habitual contacts had disappeared, and he was more astray and bewildered than any strayed dog could be.

With the passing of his people and his world his sense of identity seemed to have passed or lapsed; so that, if one had asked, he should have found it difficult to tell who he was. If one tumbled into the sea and was there questioned by fishes, what use would there be in the statement that one was, or had been, a man, with a name, and a pedigree, and a memory filled with deeds and emotions which they could not be interested in?

It seemed better that he should go into the fairy dún than that he should remain where he was to wander and stare in the fairy wilderness. Human desolation and silence he knew, but what would fairy desolation, fairy silence be like? How would he feel in fairy darkness? and what might come to him out of the unknown gloom of the Country of the Dead?

He marched, therefore, at the tail of the host, and when they reached a door set in the hillside he also went in, following the men in front of him, and keeping military pace with them.

Each man as he entered sang out cheerily:
" A man on the track here."
And the voice of a guard within replied:
" The heavier is the track."
When it came to Nera's turn, he also cried out:
" A man on the track here," and he received the reply that the others got.

CHAPTER IX

THEY went into a hill apparently, but, once entered, the hill was as translucent as air.   It ceased to be a hill.   There was no feeling or evidence of being underground, for when he looked about he saw the conditions and phenomena to which he was accustomed in the world that he had left.

Here was space and trees. Water splashed along in a moody brook, moody only, perhaps, because it was night time; and when he looked up he saw through the darkness a faint far glitter of stars, and he noted a silvery

23

radiance in the sky which might tell of an obscured moon, or might be the first delicate intimation that dawn was on the way.

He had lost count of time, and could not tell if one hour or six had elapsed since he set out on his adventure from the lawn of Cruachan.

The companies, of which he formed a part, marched along a sunken pathway arched over with trees, and this pathway wound around and about like a coiling snake.

Nera could hear the slow bubble and hush of waters coming from the right hand, but in a minute the same sound came to him from the left.

They tramped across echoes and hollownesses which told of wooden bridges under their feet, and at times they trod up high-graded, precipitate bridges of ringing stone. These sounds, and darkness, and a gleam, these made the world that ringed him in.

There was much gay talk among his companions, but it consisted mostly of allusions to which he had no clue, and the men directly in front turned now and again to stare at him with good-humoured fixity, or with quizzical or calculating eyes.

24

They came at length to the entry of a great building and marched into a courtyard surrounded on three sides by towering, battlemented walls. The courtyard was lit with innumerable torches, and at one end, on a raised dais, Ethal Anbual, the King of the Shí of Connacht, was sitting with a small group of men and women about him.

When the troops had been ranged in a semicircle about this dais, men came forward from each company carrying heads which they swung by the hair, and they laid these in order before the King, who stared fixedly at each head and demanded its name and quality.

Among the trophies Nera recognised the auburn, wide-browed head of Ailill, and the long-faced, yellow-haired head of Maeve. But he recognised each head as it was put down, and his heart nigh broke with pity for his dead companions, and with fear for himself.

When all the trophies had been ranged, the chief of the company to which he was attached beckoned to Nera and marched with him to the dais.

" What is to be done with this man? " he asked the King.

25

The King of the Shí looked steadily at him, and Nera had a confused impression of calm eyes and flashing teeth, of a long, silky, yellow beard, and of much sly amusement behind the regard that was bent on him. Several of the people on the dais leaned together whispering and laughing, and the King, bending forward with an elbow on his knee, smiled as though he divined what was being discussed behind him.

" What brought you here, my friend? " said the King.

" I came with the warriors," Nera stammered.

" That I know, but how does it happen that you have been able to leave your world and come blundering into ours? "

" I do not know how it happened," Nera replied. " All I know is that I suddenly found myself invisible to my own people, and as there seemed to be nowhere else for me to go, I came with the people of the Shí."

" It is very vexatious," said the King; " but now that you are here you must stay here, for although you have not become one of us, you have certainly ceased to be one of

26

them.   Are you prepared to work in return for your life and your food? "

" I will do anything you tell me to do."

" Very well," said the King.

CHAPTER X

THE thin radiance which he had noticed when he passed through the door of Faery did not flow from a hidden moon.   It was the faint first peeping of the dawn away on the low horizon.   And, minute by minute, that radiance spread, so that what had been a stain not bigger than a hand was now a lake flooding the eastern sky.

Nor was it any longer the colour of grey water or unpolished metal.   It was the hue of silver of great purity.   It was a tender whiteness; a spotless radiance; a deep translucency; it was a snowy immaculate loveliness, in the heart of which there grew a flush not quite to be called rose, for it was tinged with green.

In a little that flush blushed deeply, radiantly, and glowed out into gold, and by

27

these gradations the day was born and the sun began to shine.

The torches paled, for the centre of being had gone from them to where the young mild orb was climbing.

For a moment the face of the King of the Shí and the faces about him paled also; they seemed careworn, preoccupied, and pinched with a chill they had not felt before. The diadems, the carved helmets, the bronze shoulder-pieces and the shields with metal rims and bosses did not shine for that moment. They glinted, furtively, coldly, until the sun came; and then they sparkled again mellowly, friendlily, and the great yellow beard of the King foamed out in gold, and the aura about his brows took on an hundred colours.

Looking at Nera, he said thoughtfully:

" Now that you are here, I suppose you must stay here."

And Nera recognised in the word " must " a compulsion against which he was powerless; and in that moment he bade good-bye to the world he had left, and which he should see no more, or should only see as through a window.

He bade adieu to preoccupations which had been important, and were now remembered with trouble, as though they came to him from the other side of the grave. Enemies against whom he yet had a grudge he forgave. The friends with whom he had sported he blessed. And a bright-eyed girl who had glanced at him and on whom his eyes had stayed he blessed also. For all that was finished and done with, and there was no longer any meaning in such things.

He squared his shoulders, and drew into his lungs the breath of a new life, and he drew into his mind all the implications which were borne on that deep breath.

" There is a house yonder where you can stay," said the King of the Shí; " and there you will do as you are told until you have learned to do without being told."

CHAPTER XI

IT was a small dwelling, half hidden among flowering bushes.

About the door and in and out of the

windows there was the low deep hum of bees. From the sloping roof there came, in delicate monotony, the soft cooing of doves; and in the trees about there was an unceasing song, or chirp, or call, as summer birds went to and from their nests.

Within the house there was a young woman who looked on him uncritically as she received the instructions which his escort gave.

" Take care of him," said the escort, " see that he does not get lost again, for he has been badly lost already."

The young woman smiled.

" I shall see that he does not go astray," said she. " Come into the house, decent man, and rest your tiredness."

Nera went into the house, and she gave him a wooden bowl full of new milk, a slice of wheaten bread and a great piece of honey.

" That will put heart into you," she murmured.

And it did put heart into him, so that in a few minutes, as she moved about her duties, he began to look at her with an absorbed attention, and it seemed to him that having looked at her he could not want to look away again.

30

But in the middle of that gaze he fell asleep, for he was tired by the loss of his night's rest, and was yet more wearied by reason of the adventures that he had gone through and the mental disturbance to which he had been subjected.

He slept well.

The sun had climbed to the height of his course, and was beginning to descend again when Nera awakened and went out into a world so endlessly new that he could not but marvel and be delighted thereat. He felt full of joy as he walked in the garden among bees and birds and flowers, while the mild sunlight stole into and lived in him.

In the world that he had left summer had departed and all its sweets, and although winter had not come with snow and iron, it had yet ventured so many of its heralds and had blown so chill a breath that the autumn had shivered and her russet cheek had paled.

Now here was summer again, found just as he had lost it, and it was summer of a loveliness such as he had never experienced.

Here were flowers of a hue, of a sweetness, beyond all that he had seen. The sunlight

31

here was more tranquil and more rich than the light to which he was accustomed, and the breeze was freighted with such balm and spice as he could never weary of savouring.

The woman of the house called to him.

" Now you must work, sweet lad."

She gave him an axe and sent him to the wood which was at a little distance to cut down a tree. He was then to chop the wood into logs, and on the morrow he should carry these in a pannier on his back to the palace. It was only certain trees that he should cut; those which burned well and which gave out a sweet savour while burning.

It was rude work, but it did not exercise him severely, for he was very skilful with an axe. He had practised with that arm, and had been captain of a band of axemen while in the service of the King of Munster, so that once the tree came to the ground he could lop so delicately and cleave so power-fully that the work seemed almost to accomplish itself, and in small time he had amassed logs enough to fill many panniers.

In the morning he began the transport of these to the palace of Ethal Anbual.

32

CHAPTER XII

As he was returning from one of these journeys he heard two men talking as they came down a path that ran wildly among the trees.

It was a very slender, very twisting path, along which one could only see for a few yards; and it wound about so crookedly, and it was so deep in leaves, and it was so clumped and grassed and tussocked that no person could be seen or heard coming along it. Nera did not hear any step, but he caught voices, and he was so new to this country that he followed his first impulse, and striding a few paces to the side he crouched behind a tree.

A voice said:

" Will you go on, lazybones? "

And another replied:

" Lazybones yourself. I'll go on or I won't go on just as I please, but will you look out where I'm going? "

" I am looking out," the first voice said, " but you walk so slow that I want to go asleep between each step. Can't you raise

a trot out of you, lazybones?   Go six inches
to the right or you'll rub your nose off
against a tree.   Now go ahead, and foot it
out."

"Ah, it's hard to be dark, it's hard to be
dark," said the first voice.

"Ah," said the second voice, "will you
hold your prate, for I'm sick of that song.
Move twelve inches to the left, my pippin,
and go straight on.   Wait now until I duck
or I'll be scraped off by a branch.   Go ahead
and stir your stumps."

"Ah, it's hard to be dark, it's hard to be
dark," said the first voice.

"Can't you say something besides that?"
the other cried.

"I can't, and I won't.   I'll say it's hard
to be dark, it's hard to be dark until I die,
and I'll say it when I'm dead, and I'll say it
after I'm dead."

"You'll die now," his companion roared,
"if you don't take two steps to the left and
one to the right."

Nera peeped, and saw the two who were
coming.   One was mounted on the shoulders
of the other.   The man who was on top had
no legs, and Nera saw that the man who was

34

walking had no eyes.   The blind man acted as legs to the lame man and the latter acted as eyes to the blind man.

Nera followed, for he wondered where they were going, and admired the manner in which they had doubled their abilities and halved their troubles.   After a while they turned from the path and went where a smaller track ran among trees.   In a little they came to a well, and the blind man halted, leaning against the well, while the lame man stared into it.

" Is it there, my soul? " said the blind man testily.

" It is," his companion replied.

" Very well," said the other, " let us get out of this, for my back is broken, so it is. Ah, it's hard to be dark, it's hard to be dark."

" Will you hold your tongue? " the cripple snarled.

" I won't," the blind man screamed. " I'll say, it's hard to be dark until Doom, and I'll say it afterwards as well."

" Go nine inches to the left," his companion roared, " or you're done for, for there's a rock in the way will split your shin

35

and crack your skull and dinge your stomach, and kill the pair of us."

The blind man trod a careful nine inches.

" Am I to go on now? " said he, " or what am I to do? Can't you mind where I'm going? "

" Amn't I minding it, lazybones. Will you go on ten steps, and then——"

" Ah, it's hard to be dark, it's hard to be dark," cried the blind man, and then they turned among trees and disappeared.

Nera went home in a tranquil, dewy eve.

The sun had been steadily declining. Now, but one red shoulder of the Titan rested on the dreaming slope ; and from it there came a beam rosy and gentle as the light we imagine in dream.

Still from the roof-tree came the faint, intermittent moaning of the doves : so low the ear must wait to catch it; and at times so low it seemed but as a surmise in the heart, as though the air itself cooed gently at long and longer intervals. A lazy hum stayed for one long instant in the air as a late bee, gorged with sweets, took the way of content homewards. From the trees near by there came but a sound or two, a chirp of welcome or inquiry, and a swift whirr as wings flew into and folded among the leaves.

And as he stood in the last faint beam, no longer red but brown, he thought of the friends that he had left, so long ago it seemed, and that they all were dead, and he thought how that dear world was lost to him for ever.

He went sadly into the house then, and the sweet-cheeked, honey-haired woman set before him bread and meat and honey, with a bubbling mether of new, sweet milk, and a great horn filled with wine; and in partaking of this food, and in the regard of that quiet-eyed companion he forgot his friends and comrades, and the disasters that had over-taken them, and the plight in which he was.

CHAPTER XIII

HE stayed for a long time talking, for he was loath to leave her for his couch, and she was as unwilling to let him go.

37

" Tell me, Woman of the House, what is really the life in this world? "

" We wish, and what we wish we get."

" Do you get all that you wish for? "

" Only the simple things. Things to eat and to wear; sunlight and sweet scents. Every person gets what he is able to wish for, but the power of every person to wish is different."

" You, for instance, O honey-haired companion! what do you get? "

" What I can wish for," she answered with a smile.

" Are you not easily satisfied? " said Nera, looking on the neat and pleasant but poor interior.

" Before I came here from the world of mortal men," said she, " I had small peace, and it will take a long time before I grow discontented with this quiet happiness."

" Also," she continued smilingly: " I do not yet know how to wish powerfully and grandly as the King does and as others do, for I am not educated in these things; therefore, I only have what I can wish for, and am contented. I shall get other things when I learn the way to want them."

"I know what I want," cried Nera
roguishly.

"If you know that, you will certainly get
it," she answered, and her eyes rested on him
gently as the cooing of the doves had rested
on the rosy air.

"Tell me more of these things," said Nera,
"for I could listen to your voice for ever."

"This world is called Tir na n-Óg, the
Land of the Young. It is within the world
you have left, as an apple is within its skin,
and all who die in your world come to this
one. But within this world there is another
called the Land of Wonders, and those who
die here, or who can wish to do so, go to the
Land of Wonders. Within the Land of
Wonders there is yet a world called the Land
of Promise, and those who die in the Land of
Wonders are born into the Land of Promise,
but they cannot die there until they can wish
to do so."

"And after the Land of Promise?"

"After the Land of Promise there is your
world again."

"All this is very wonderful," said Nera.
"Are there any other things that you can
tell me?"

"In the world you come from," she continued, "time moves slowly, but in this world it goes yet slower."

"I do not understand that at all," cried Nera.

"Nothing is real here, for everything is wished, so that here a minute is like a day, time moves so slowly with us and we live so quickly. In the Land of Wonders time moves yet more slowly and life goes faster, so in that land a minute is like a thousand years. And in the Land of Promise time ceases entirely and there is only life."

"These are hard sayings," said Nera. "I do not comprehend them."

"I do not understand them well either," she replied; "but that is what we are taught."

"Still," said Nera, "there is something that I do comprehend."

"And what is that?" she inquired.

"That I adore you," said he.

As she made no reply he strode to her and gave her three kisses.

"You must not do that," said she, "for Ethal Anbual has not given permission."

"But since it is my wish," said Nera.

40

" Since it is our wish," he continued tenderly.
" Do you not wish it also? " he asked.

She smiled at him, as one surprised and
delighted:

" Indeed I did not know that I wished it,"
said she, and placing her arms about his neck
she gave him three gentle kisses.

CHAPTER XIV

ALL the next day he was busy cutting and
carrying wood.

He had no desire for companions, and did
not meet any. He only saw those in the
palace to whom he delivered the timber,
and as his work needed no explanation he
did not enter into talk with them. A few
people went by him among the offices; some
hurrying servants, some agile and laughing
children, but all that he passed with these
was the word of blessing, which is the word
of greeting.

" God to you," he said.

" God be with the work," they answered.

At times, as he went to and fro, there came

from the farther side of the palace a great blowing of bugles. At times a body of armed men marched past him with rhythmic step and fierce, alert faces. Or a cloud of horsemen, with a gallant shining of shields and spears and a great clashing of accoutrement, went galloping by.

Saving for these, his marchings were as solitary as though he moved through a desert, and his true companion was the sunlight that danced among the leaves or the cool shadows that slept behind tree and rock.

He had leisure, so, to consider the things he had been told of, and to make some attempts at wishing.

If his opinion had been sought, Nera would have said that to wish is an ideal occupation for an idle man, and one which called for no particular endowment. But he now discovered that what he had regarded as wishing was merely a lax wandering of the mind; a superficial fancying in which, although his sympathies were engaged, his mind or will was quiescent. He tried to wish, but found that he did not know how to do it, for when one image formed in his mind, another

42

succeeded to it before the first had received
one-half its due attention.

He found, also, that he did not know what
to wish for. He had food in abundance,
there were sunshine and sweet airs about
him, and no person interfered with him.
His health was perfect, and his strength was
equal to any call that could reasonably be
made upon it.

He was a little bewildered.

" Is there nothing I lack? " he cried. And
he sat upon a moss-grown trunk to consider
this matter.

He could not consider it cogently, for his
mind would run to the world that he had
left, calling up faces, characters, events,
about which it warned him also that he
need be no more exercised. Ambitions had
been his in that world, but in this one they
did not seem to have any relevancy.

What did it now matter that his comrade
Cairbre might take his place as captain of a
troop? And it was likely, moreover, that
his comrade Cairbre was dead, and that the
troop was stretched with him in equal chilly
stiffness.

" They are dead," he thought, " or they

will shortly die; and I," he thought again, in a flash of amazement that was also terror, " and I can never die, for I am dead now, and I am yet as alive as I have ever been or ever can be."

The thought terrified and sobered and steadied him.

" I must learn more of this world," he thought, " and find out what in it is worth attention."

And then he remembered that dove-eyed companion who was waiting for him where birds were singing, where the bees went in contentment. And he knew that he lacked nothing which she could not give, and that he need wish for no more than the joys of which she was mistress.

Her tranquil eyes; her cool and tender hands; her breast that could woo him to rest and rest again, and could quit him of that weariness which had gathered with the years. There he could forget all the effort and agitation which had been that which he once thought of as life.

He arose joyful, impatient, full of desire and eagerness, and, swinging the axe lustily as he strode, he took his way to that house of dream.

44

CHAPTER XV

HE was welcomed there, and as he took his dear mistress in his arms he felt that there was nothing more to be wished for, and that his hands were holding all that existence had to offer of tempting or satisfactory.

After they had eaten, he began to ask questions, for he was yet full of curiosity; and he loved, furthermore, to look on her lips as they moved and shaped words. He loved to hear the delicate sweet sound of these words as she uttered them, and to look in her eyes as they widened and narrowed, and as they shaded or emphasised her thought.

He told her of the men he had seen on the previous day, one mounted on the shoulders of the other, one of them being without legs, while the other was without sight, and he begged that she should tell him the meaning of this collaboration, and of that journey.

She informed him that these were men who guarded certain treasures belonging to the King of the Shí, notably the Crown of Bruin, the Mantle of Laery, and the Shirt

45

of Dunlaing.   That nobody knew where the
treasures were hidden except these two and
the King, and that it was a strange accident
he should have come on them while they
were making their visit of duty.

"But why should the King choose such
curious guards for his treasure?" he asked.

"They cannot steal it, for they cannot run
away.   The one is too blind to see the
treasure and so he cannot get it.   The other
can see the treasure, but as he has no legs he
cannot get away with it."

"But," Nera objected, "they might tell
a third person, an evil comrade, and he could
take the treasure.   They," said he, for he
lived hopefully, "they could tell me, and I
have all the legs and eyes that any one could
need."

"No," she replied, "they will not tell any
one else.   These men covet the treasure and
they will tell no one about it.   They wish for
treasure, and in a way they have it, but they
have wished themselves into slavery to get it."

"It seems to me," said Nera, "that one's
wish does not always turn out as one wished."

"You must not desire a thing which be-
longs to another person," she answered, "for

46

then there are two wishes, each acting against the other, and the people who are thus covetous are left in an unsatisfactory middle place which is torment."

" I see that it is of no use to wish at all," cried Nera discontentedly.

" Yes," she replied, " you may desire things which everybody can enjoy with you, and that is true wishing."

" Such things as——? " said Nera scornfully.

" Sunlight and the song of birds, good food and health, a contented mind and a good understanding. These hurt no one, and every one is the better for possessing them, or for living among people who have them."

Nera revolved these thoughts, but it seemed to him that they were not profitable, for he considered that the things worth having were those which other people owned or lacked, and he thought there was small value in possessions which anybody might enjoy who cared to want them.

CHAPTER XVI

BUT suddenly the young man's face went purple and he smote the table a blow with his fist, so that everything on it went jigging up and down, and his companion leaped in surprise.

"What is it, my lamb, my little calf?" said she, and she ran to him.

"I know what I wish for," cried Nera triumphantly, furiously.

"What is it?" she whispered.

"I want the prize I won; I have been cheated out of my prize," he cried savagely.

"But what prize are you speaking of? Who has dared to cheat you?"

"My gold-hilted sword," he cried. "The blade that Ailill dared me to win, and which I won."

And as he said these words a terrible despair came on him, the light turned grey before his eyes, and he beat his fists together.

"Tell me about your prize," she pleaded.

And she pressed a soft hand over his forehead, and she kissed his eyelids tenderly.

48

" Tell me all that happened to you," she urged.

So Nera sat again in his chair, and looking backwards in memory and in the world that he had left, he arranged his thoughts and began to tell of his adventures.

His companion listened, wide-eyed, while he told of the wager that Ailill had made, and of the dreadful night through which her beloved had passed.

" And now," he concluded, " I can never get my prize, for I have strayed away from that world. Noble Ailill and Maeve of the Long White Cheek are dead, and all who were with them have been slaughtered."

But at this his lady began to laugh, and her merriment was so infectious that, in his own despite, Nera laughed with her, but he was hurt also.

" What is there in my story to make you happy? " he inquired.

" It is all a mistake," she murmured, wiping the tears of laughter from her eyes.

" What is all a mistake? "

" They are not dead," she replied.

" But I saw the slaughter with these same eyes which are now marvelling at you. I

49   E

saw Ailill lying outside the tent with a broken sword in his hand, and I looked down on Maeve lying inside the tent, all doubled up, and all in and out of blood."

" Nevertheless——"

" And, after that, I saw men swinging up the heads of my companions for the King of the Shí to look at."

" It was only a game," she cried.

" A game!   Alas!   that game went against my comrades."

" You will not listen," she cried, beating her hands together.   " It was a game, it was not real."

" It was not real! " he murmured, staring at her.   " I no longer understand anything, and you are right to laugh at me."

" You will understand," she cried, " if you will only listen."

" Very good," said Nera, " I will listen, but I am perfectly certain that I shall not understand, for I saw their heads swinging by the hair while the King of the Shí stared at them."

" It was not real.   It did not happen."

" Whether it happened or whether it did not happen I saw it happening," said Nera stubbornly.

" I shall beat you," she cried, " if you do not listen to me."

" I am listening indeed," he replied, " my ears are waggling," said he.

" The King of the Shí was angry because of a thing Maeve did long ago, when she helped Angus of the Brugh to take a girl out of Faery, out of this very Shí of Connacht."

" I heard of that.   So far I am sane."

" And so the King wished to make war on Maeve, and his wish was fulfilled in his world, but it was not fulfilled in her world."

" Very good, and what follows from that?"

" It follows that Maeve is not dead, and that Ailill is not dead, and that all the companions you left alive are just as living as when you left them."

CHAPTER XVII

" I shall awaken soon," said Nera, " for I surely must be asleep and dreaming."

" You saw a wish being fulfilled," she continued, " and as a wish is formed in the mind, so it must be satisfied in the mind; and as

51

this is the first world of the mind, and as you strayed into it, you have seen something happening which happened in the mind, and did not happen anywhere else."

" My mind is about to slip out through my ears and leave my head empty."

" It is quite plain," she insisted.

" Doubtless it is. But I begin to understand that I shall never again understand anything. Alas! alas!" said he, " I have become a fool, and I may go mad presently and bite people on the leg."

But his lovely companion interrupted him soothingly: " Ailill and Maeve and all your companions are alive, for this time," she said.

" For this time?" said Nera. " I am beginning again to wonder, and I cannot stand too much astonishment, for it makes my head buzz."

" A thing," said she, " can be conceived and exercised in the mind, but when it has been so exercised in the mind that it really becomes real there, it then becomes real in every part of nature and in all the worlds where life is living."

" In good truth . . .!" said Nera.

" It is by this wishing and willing that the worlds are made, and that everything is made."

" I will let these things pass," said Nera, " for I perceive that I am not intelligent. But what did you mean by saying that Maeve and Ailill are safe ' for this time '? "

" This time," said she, " the King of the Shí has rehearsed mentally something which may become real the next time he tries to do it. It was so nearly real this time that you were able to see it happening. It will be so real the next time that it will happen, and the Queen of Connacht will die with many of her people unless they are warned, and can pit their wish against our wish; for we, be sure of it, will all wish together."

" And if they can do that? "

" If they can do that, nothing will happen."

" Can they do it? " he asked.

" There are wise poets and magicians in Cruachan," she replied. " Where there is a poet there is a wish, and where there is a magician there is a will."

" Tell me this also," said Nera, " when does the King of the Shí mean to attack Cruachan? "

" On next Samhain, for at the Feast of Samhain the doors between this world and that world are opened, and those who desire to do so can pass from the one place to the other."

Nera beat his hands together.

" There is no hope," he cried, " for until next Samhain we cannot get out to give them warning, and it will then be too late."

" Do you greatly desire to do that? " she asked.

" By my hand, I do."

" Then," said she, " you can do it."

" But Samhain is past," said Nera.

" It is not past," she said.

CHAPTER XVIII

" DEAR heart," said Nera, " you must bear with me, and forgive me, for I feel in my bones that I am overflowing with stupidity, and that the only words I shall henceforth utter will be words like ' why ' and ' what ' and the other ones that are used in front of

54

questions. Tell me what you meant when you said they will not be attacked until next Samhain, and that this Samhain has not yet passed."

" I mean exactly that," she replied. " How long have you been here? "

Nera looked at her.

" I must think, lest I say something foolish —I have been here for three days."

" That is according to our time," she agreed. " But according to the time in your world, how long have you been here? "

" Three days."

" No," she said. " You have been here three minutes, for a minute of your time is a day of ours."

" Then," cried Nera, starting up, " this is still Samhain."

" It is."

" How long," she continued, " did it take you to go from the lawn of Cruachan to the hill where the outlaws were hanged? "

" Five minutes."

" And from there back again (for all the rest was magic) five minutes, and you have been three minutes here. The meal which was being prepared when you went away is

55

not yet on the board; Ailill and Maeve are now looking for your return, and you have been absent from Cruachan exactly thirteen minutes."

Nera leaped again from his seat.

" I shall get my sword," he cried. " Tell me," he whispered urgently, " how shall I leave Faery? "

" Would you indeed leave me? " she pleaded, and the tears welled in her eyes and overflowed upon her cheeks.

But he seized her hands:

" I shall return," he promised her. " I could not now exist without you, but I must get the prize I won, or I shall never know happiness again; and I must warn the poets of Connacht of what may happen next Samhain. Tell me, O my dear heart and my one treasure, how can I leave Faery? "

" You will come back? "

" I will surely return," said he; " I swear by the powers of the elements and by the gods of my people that I will surely return."

" Then," said she, " I will tell you. You have only to go back the way you came. The door in the hill is open, for this is the night of Samhain, and when you pass through the door you will pass into the world you came from."

" But Maeve will not believe what I tell her," he cried lamentably. " She will say I am inventing a tale."

" Take fruits of summer with you," she counselled.

" That is a good idea," he agreed, and he breathed at last easily and calmly.

They went to the door then, and she gathered wild garlic and primrose and golden fern, and she put these into his hand, looking at him closely and sorrowfully as she gave the flowers.

But he was thinking of the way he had come; of the winding road that passed over rocky bridges and little bridges of wood, and that took its course in loops and twists and winding ways, with the sound of water brawling now on the one side and again babbling from the other.

" I must go," said Nera, " for I shall have a long journey before I come to the door in the hill."

" It will take a full quarter of a minute of your time," said she.

They kissed each other tenderly then, and parted.

" You will come back to me? " she called.

" I will surely come back," he called in reply.

CHAPTER XIX

HE set out then, and at the bend of the road he halted to look back at the little house bowered among trees and flowering shrubs.

The late sunlight, half gold, half rose, was drowsing peacefully about it, and in the ear of memory he could hear the call and answer as dove murmured to dove from the roof-tree, and the drone of bees as they passed and re-passed the windows.

He saw his delicious mate standing at the end of the little path that ran to the house, and they waved a hand to each other once, twice, and thrice.

Then he stepped aside into the wood bordering the roadway and set across to where the palace lay, and where the road began that went in loops and curls uphill and down; and so to the sunken path which ran under an arch of trees, and thus to the door in the hillside, and the world of men.

It was a long journey, but he beguiled it by thinking of what he was coming from and where he was going to; by thinking of the gold-hilted blade which would leave a King's side to be strapped on his own lean thigh. And he remembered her also, the honey-haired, the delicious; his comely mate, his tender-handed comrade; but when he had half turned to go back to her he remembered the evil which must fall on Connacht, and he remembered again the golden-hilted sword which he had won but had not got; and so he marched again, impatient, bewildered, tormented.

When he came nigh the end of his journey, the day, too, had ended. There was but a fleck of colour here and there on the western sky, and as he went these paled or sank below the horizon, so that when he reached the path arched over with trees all that daylight had gone, and he had to walk carefully lest he should strike against one of the trees which he could no longer see.

"I shall not know if I am in or out of the door," he thought, "this darkness is so profound. But," he also thought, " I must be close to it now, for I do not hear the river which I began to hear when I had marched a few minutes' distance from the door the last time."

He stood to listen, and was satisfied that no river was near him. He could hear nothing and see nothing, for the darkness and the silence were of equal unmitigated depth, and each seemed to be portion of the other.

He went forward again, and after a few stumbling paces a voice spoke, which brought him standing stiff as a tree-trunk.

" Who comes? " said the voice.

He remembered the words that had passed when he entered, and replied in these words.

" A man on the track here," he called.

" The heavier is the track," the voice replied jovially.

In two paces he passed the place whence the voice came from, and knew that he was through the door of Faery, and that he was back in the world of men.

CHAPTER XX

Now he knew where he was.

He started to run in the direction of the lawn of Cruachan, and although he stumbled and fell, bruising himself against the rocks, and tearing his hands among the bracken, he yet continued to run, for he was wonderfully excited by the adventures he had passed through, and he wished with all his heart to look on men once more.

Hurrying thus he came to the skirt of the lawn, and outside the circle of lights cast by the torches he stood to compose himself, and to gaze. For it did not seem credible that what he saw was true, and yet what he did see was so precise that he could not deny the evidence of his eyes.

Everything was as it had been when he went from the lawn to the hill of execution.

The torches were casting long golden flames among the branches of the tree, and the fire in front of the tent was tossing tongues of gold into the air. Ailill, the King, was stretched in the opening of the tent, and was still gazing out upon the darkness as

61

though he were trying to pierce it with a profound meditation; and other people, men and women and servants, were moving peacefully or busily about the tent.

Nera stepped from the shadows, and as he advanced Ailill saw him and called out a welcome and a greeting.

"Well, my dear heart, so you did come back?"

"I have come for my prize," said Nera with sober excitement.

"You shall have it with my love, but you must tell us all that happened, for I perceive that something has happened."

"No, no," cried Maeve, "if there is a story to be told——"

"There is a story indeed," Nera interposed, and he laid into the King's hand wild garlic and primroses and golden fern.

"By my soul . . .!" said the King, staring, astounded, on a vanished summer.

" . . . It must not be told during the feast," Maeve continued, "but at the banquet which will follow the feast, we can listen to it while we drink the royal liquors that I have provided."

While she spoke the servers and butlers

came into the tent bearing mighty dishes and baskets, and the steam which arose from those dishes lent such a savour to the air that the tongues of every person present darted across their lips, and they moved with one accord towards the benches and tables which were ranged about the great tent.

It was a mighty and a glorious feast, and all that Maeve had said about it beforehand was surpassed, for she had not enumerated one-half of her bounty nor extolled in anything like measure the potency of her mead and wine.

When the feast was ended the banquet began, and when all present had been supplied with the drink they loved best, Ailill called to Nera:

"Come beside us on the dais, my darling, for I am sure that you have strange things to tell."

Nera went on the dais then, and he was given a great four-handed mether filled with ale, and when he had drunk to the health of Maeve and Ailill and to the health of the noble company, the mether was refilled for him, and he drunk from it to his own satisfaction.

63

Then he commenced to tell of his adventures.

As he spoke, silence grew about the tent, and in a little time each person was leaning forward staring at him. The silence was so profound that if a pin had fallen each person present would have heard it, and frowned angrily. They forgot the ale as they listened; they forgot the sweet mead, and the glowing wine that had come from distant countries; and they hung on his words as though they had ceased to be men and women, and had become ears only.

When he had made an end to the tale a great sigh went through the tent, and then each person drank soberly from the methers and goblets which were before them, and they seemed to be sunken in a maze that was one-half astonishment and one-half reverie.

" It is a lovely story," said Maeve, " and I should willingly listen to it again."

" But I also," she continued, smiling on Nera, " am honey-haired, and there are some who think that I am sweet-cheeked and desirable."

Ailill sighed also, and stood up. He unstrapped the gold-hilted blade as he spoke:

64

" Good my soul," he said, " you have won your prize, and no better man will ever wear this sword than the man I am giving it to."

" Nay," cried Maeve indignantly, " it is I that shall give Nera the sword, for it is I am the Queen of Connacht and the giver of gifts in this country."

She took the sword from her husband, and she gazed so kindly on Nera that he was embarrassed and did not know where he should look. Then she strapped the weapon about his waist. As she bent beside him the scent from her hair and from her white shoulders came to him, but although he was moved and happy thereat, it was not of Maeve he thought while he stared down upon her noble head; he thought of the delicious, smiling comrade who was waiting for him in Tir na n-Óg, counting the days and watching for his return from the door of a sun-steeped cottage.

" So," said Ailill thoughtfully, " the King of the Shí of Uaman thinks he can destroy Connacht! We shall be prepared for that person next Samhain."

" I shall march into his Shí, as I marched before," said Maeve fiercely, " and when I

65   F

quit it this time there will be little left for Ethal Anbual to reign over."

"When did you attack the Shí of Crua-chan?" Fergus inquired, "I have never heard of that sacking."

"You shall hear it now," Maeve returned, "for I will tell you the story myself."

She sat in the great seat then, and drank a little goblet of mead, and the Bell-Branch was rung so that the company again went silent.

CHAPTER XXI

SAID Maeve:

In the days that are past and gone, Angus mac an Óg, the son of the Dagda Mór, was resting at the Brugh.

He had the gift of perpetual youth, and was therefore called the mac an Óg—The Son of the Two Young Ones. He had the gift of perpetual beauty, and was so called The Wonder; and he had the gift of magic, and was known by it as The Envious.

When he went abroad there accompanied him a cloud of birds that wheeled and sang

66

about his head, so that when we see a cloud of wheeling and singing birds, all frantic with energy and exultation, we know that the son of the Dagda is passing, and we make obeisance to Youth and Beauty and Magic.

It happened that Angus was staying at his father's palace, the Brugh of the Boyne, in the Shí of Ulster, for he had not yet cozened his father out of this palace. There had been a feast that night, with a banquet after the feast, and the time had passed in music and singing, and in the recitation of their verse by poets.

After the banquet, Angus went to bed, but he could not sleep. He lay looking on the darkness of his chamber, wondering why he was wakeful, and finding no reason for it. For he was in good health and spirits, and nothing had occurred to disturb his mind.

" Some one," he thought, " is practising a magical art against me, and but that I do not wish to get out of bed I would weave magic also and destroy that influence, or I should find out where it comes from."

" And indeed," he thought also, " if I cannot go to sleep it is no great calamity, for

I have slept many times and shall sleep many a time again."

While he was thus considering, the room lightened, and he saw a figure standing at a little distance from the bed. The young god raised himself on his elbow and looked intently on the figure.

He knew it was not real, because real things do not happen in this way: he knew it was not a dream, because he was awake; and he knew, therefore, that this must be a vision, or the wraith of a person come to visit him.

But the figure did not speak, nor did Angus.

They but looked at, and recognised each in the other the extreme and goal of all that was lovely in the world.

Angus sunk himself in that gaze, as a fish is immersed in water. He forgot all but the delicious face on which he was gazing. He forgot that this was but a vision; and he could only remember to look and look again, and to so concentrate his sight that he could see not only with his eyes, but with every member of his being, and with all the faculties of his mind.

68

He was lost in that look and drowned in it, so that when the vision faded he could not withdraw his eyes from that rigid forwardness and contemplation.

But the darkness did at last cloud his mind and enable him to withdraw his faculties and to become master of himself.

He sank back on the bed, full of joy, full of wonder and surmise, with his heart hurried by such happiness that it nigh broke from his bosom; and for a long time he lay in the stillness and darkness reconstructing a beauty such as even he had never contemplated before.

The hours of the long night passed for him in an ecstasy of wonder, in a recollection that was all happiness. But when the pale wraith of day began to move through the room, so that all things looked uncertain and discoloured, his mood changed with the change that came to his eyes, and he began to remember that he did not know who had come to him, that he did not know where that lovely being might be, nor could he tell if she who had appeared would ever appear to him again.

For he knew that things which begin in one place can have their sequel in another, and may end far from either; and that the whole story may be unknown to any person except that lonely soul which is fulfilling itself in its own experiences.

Therefore, when he left the bed he left it weariedly, and his bearing was so depressed that all the people of the Shí noticed it, and at last his mother noticed it also.

His mother was Boann,[1] the wife of the Great Good God.

CHAPTER XXII

She questioned him, but as his replies were evasive or distraught, she gave up a fruitless inquiry and sought elsewhere for a solution of her son's trouble.

It was a trouble indeed.   He fell sick of it, and would not talk to nor look at any one, nor would he reply to any person who addressed him.

He might glance for a moment on the questioner as though wondering why an inquisitive person should be in the room with

---

[1] Boann = The River Boyne.

him, and then he would turn his eyes aside and stare, far away in space, at something seen only by himself.

The physicians of the Shí were brought, but against his obstinate silence they could do nothing, for they did not seem to exist for him, and he himself did not seem to exist in the world where they were real.

Among these there was a physician whose name was Fergne.

He was a clever doctor. Not only did he understand the afflictions which the body may endure, he was versed also in those ills which come to the body from the mind; and when he had been with Angus for a little time he knew that, however bad his health might seem, the reason was not physical.

He spoke to Angus, and by dint of much speaking he insisted in time on being listened to.

" You know, Angus, dear heart, no one should lie in bed whose body is as healthy as yours is, and what I think is, that there must be a trouble in your mind which is drawing the energy from your limbs, and which will drain all virtue out of you unless you make a stand against it."

71

He went then and told Angus's mother.

"The boy is in love. That is all that's wrong with him."

"But he always is in love," cried Boann; "love is his normal condition."

"It is his normal condition to have love given to him," replied Fergne; "but this time some one is withholding love from him, and he is sick from desire and dissatisfaction."

Boann and Fergne then returned to where Angus was:

"Brightness of my heart," said Boann severely, "we know what is wrong with you."

He smiled a scornful disbelief at that.

"You are not sick at all," said his mother; "you are in love."

And then, for those in love are convinced that all other people are foolish, Angus did not smile any longer. He looked admiringly at his mother and admitted that she had told the truth.

Then, for one discovered in love can no longer be silent about it, he told her of the vision which had come to him on the night of the banquet, and how, such was his trance of amazement and delight, he had let it go;

72

and he told that he would die unless he saw the girl again; and he so told and retold these things that his mother had to stop him from any more tellings.

"Darling," she said, "I know all the women of Ireland, but I do not know one who resembles in any way the person you describe."

But Fergne declared that the mac an Óg had given a full description of every woman in the world, and he developed this theme to Angus.

"If your fawn had a hump on her back, or a lame leg. If she were one-eyed or covered with warts. If she were even a lunatic, or out-and-out mad, we should have something to look for.

"But," he continued, to Boann, "it is an endless chase that we are asked to go on; and, as an endless chase is a chase without an end, it is useless to begin it."

They heard then that the Dagda had returned from his visit to the Provincial Shís of Ireland, so Boann and Fergne went to him, and described the condition of his son, and how no one could tell what should be done.

CHAPTER XXIII

THE Dagda Mór considered the extraordinary position.

" Angus does not know who the girl is? " he inquired.

" He does not."

" If he knew," the Dagda continued, " we could pick his brain and take the information from it; but, as nobody knows, why, there is no brain to pick, and I do not see what can be done. The boy has managed to get sick by himself, he must manage to get well by himself."

" There is nothing wiser than that to be said," Fergne agreed.

But Boann was not satisfied.

" We must do something," she insisted.

" Make a suggestion," said the Dagda.

Boann then suggested that the Dagda should send visions to Angus of all the beautiful women of the Shí of Ireland; and, if that failed, of all the beautiful women of Ireland itself.

" It is a lengthy and cumbersome arrangement," quoth the Dagda.

74

" Can you suggest a better one?" she asked.

But he could not do so; and it was arranged that the experiment should be tried.

" I must be in the room passing the visions before him," said the Dagda, " so that when he recognises his beloved we shall know which of them it is, for the boy has become feather-brained, and might forget which woman of the sequence was the one he sought, and it would all have to be done again."

" And I," said Boann, " will be present also, for I should like to know which woman of the women of Ireland could make anybody sick for lack of her."

" I," Fergne cried gleefully, " will attend those visions with you, for there is nothing I like better than looking at pretty women, and this time I may see my fill of them."

The Dagda was considering:

" In what order and precedence should these ladies be presented?" he inquired.

" Queens first," replied Boann, " and then Princesses who are rulers of territories, and next Princesses of birth, and then Princesses of beauty, and after them——"

" I do not like that way. We should

75

arouse the rage and jealousy of all the women of the Shí, for not one of them would be satisfied with the precedence allotted to her, except the very first one of all. Make another suggestion."

" Let them go in order of age," she advised.

" They are all twenty years of age," the Dagda mused, " and whoever denied that of any one of them would make a mortal enemy of that one. Make another suggestion."

" I can't," sighed Boann.

" Have you a suggestion? " he demanded of Fergne.

" I have, indeed."

" Then let us hear it," cried the Dagda.

" This is my suggestion," said Fergne: " Let the women be marshalled in the visions according to fatness and thinness; the fat beauties pacing before Angus according to their varying fatnesses, and the slender heroines moving before him in a diminishing scale."

" And when we come to the ones that are too thin to be seen? " the Dagda queried.

" These doves need not be shown at all," Fergne replied.

76

" There will yet be a question," the Dagda
continued, " as to whether this one is as fat
as this one, or whether this one is as slim as
that? "

" Then let those dainty ones be marshalled
according to colour; the golden-haired, winsome enchantresses marching before Angus
according as their hair is the colour of old
gold or new; the proud dark-haired fawns
moving in the like descending gradations;
the brown-haired doves following in graded
beautiful battalions; and the ardent red-
haired sorceresses keeping their own brisk
companies."

" It is a good advice," said the Dagda,
" and that is the way I shall do it."

CHAPTER XXIV

THIS scheme was explained to Angus, and
he agreed that it should be tried. But he
was so anxious to see the girl again that
he would have tested any scheme which
promised to revive that loveliness.

He was ashamed, too, that he, the Master

of Magic, could have been taken at unawares, and should have been so stupefied by any occurrence that he could neglect the very primaries and school-texts of his art; and he knew that the lady who was concerned would not easily forgive that carelessness.

He settled himself, therefore, to observe the visions.

His mother sat at one side of the couch; Fergne sat at the other, and at the head of the couch, between it and the wall, his father sat.

" When you see the lovely one you want, cry Hola," said the Dagda.

Angus Óg nodded comprehension.

" I," said Fergne, " shall look very particularly at that one."

By the power of the Dagda the sunlight which was pouring into the room faded and disappeared, and for a moment they sat in darkness.

Then the darkness glowed to a light that was like molten gold, with, seen far through it, a haze of purple, and while they stared through the golden radiance and at the purple haze, a figure moved out of the haze and stood in the golden light, and it seemed indeed as if the light flowed from her, so beautiful and proud was she, and it seemed also that if she retired the world would go black for lack of her.

"That is Fand, daughter to Bove, the King of the Shí of the Men of Femen," said Boann.

"Whether this be the right one or the wrong one," said Fergne, "what I counsel is, that Angus should take this one quickly, for, by my hand, there can be nothing more beautiful than she is under the eye of day."

But Angus made no remark and the vision faded.

"This one," Boann commented, "is Ailne of the White Shoulder, a Princess from the Shí of Leinster."

"She is lovely as a rose," said Fergne, "she is healthy as a trout, and sweet flavoured as an autumn nut. If Angus is not satisfied with this fawn it is because nothing will satisfy him."

"And this one," said Boann, "is ruler over the Shí of Meath."

"She is a joy for ever," Fergne cried.

79

" She cannot be beaten, and she is the very girl that Angus craves for."

" Do you let this dove pass? " he cried reproachfully as the next vision came. " Will you blink at the Pearl of the World? "

But Angus did let her go.

" Now," Fergne said, " you will cry Hola: now you will surely say, this is the Queen."

And after that, in despair, Fergne ceased to importune him.

CHAPTER XXV

" I PERCEIVE," said the physician, " that you have begun with the plump women, and I perceive also that of created beings a well-rounded woman overtops all others, for she can set the heart at ease and fill the mind with fancy."

" There is," he said later, " much to be said of slender women; they have a grace of movement that is infinitely satisfying; they curve and flow."

" How agile the thin maidens are! " he

murmured thoughtfully. " How deep is the appeal of their willowy youth! "

" But," he said again, " golden-haired is the one colour for women: only with gold are they adequately crowned."

" And yet," he murmured, " how winsome brown hair can be! What a shy sparkle lies in the braided tress, and how tenderly it finds the heart! "

" Noble," he asserted, " noble is the darkness piled above the dawn: majestic are the black-haired heroines; full of frolic and loveliness are they of the fragrant locks."

" To the red-haired queens I give the palm," he cried; " they warm the world; they are the true Honey of Delight."

The visions came and went, and Angus stared in a fever of hope and despair on each.

Ladies of all ages were there, from the wild young fawn of fifteen years to the massive and magnificent dame of forty.

There were ladies of a royal fatness who moved vehemently upon the vision as a great ship, with all sail spread, bears mightily down the sea.

There were others, plump as corn-fed pigeons, active as hares, raising the wind as they passed and lifting the soul to journey with them.

And others again, vehement and bewitching, moving like fierce swans upon the water.

Eyes looked upon Angus that were proud and radiant.   Eyes that were meek as doves or soft as the glance of a doe.   Sparkling and forward-looking eyes stared from the vision as an eagle stares hardily on the sun. Eyes that were languishing and appealing. Side-sliding eyes.   Eyes that tantalised. Eyes that shone with mischief, or stared with stubborn pride.   Eyes that promised and appealed and dared and cajoled; and eyes that were contented or indifferent or curious.

They came and went, and as each came, Boann named her name and Fergne murmured a benediction.

" Here," he would say, " is a dove to satisfy even the mac an Óg."

Or:

" This is the Cluster of Nuts.   This is the True Blossom of the Branches."

Or:

" To this one I give the palm, for she is surely the Berry of the Mountain."

Or again he would say:

" Now cry Hola, for here is the Star of the Bright Dawn; here is the Loveliness that Broods above the Day."

But Angus took no heed of these admonishments, except that at times he gave a groan, and, at times again, he sighed as though his heart had come and gone upon a bubble of air.

For a year and a day the visions continued, and at the end of that time the women of all the Shís of Ireland had been shown to Angus, and all the women of Ireland had been discovered to him as well.

The wives and daughters of Princes, the winsome consorts of ruling Chieftains, and the dear companions of Champions and Dragons of the Gael were brought before him; but among them he did not discover her for whom he sought; so that when the visions were ended he closed his eyes and lay back upon the bed, and he was delivered to a silence and despair twice as great as that in which he had been beforetime plunged.

CHAPTER XXVI

" I CAN do no more," said the Dagda.

" Nor could any one," Fergne interposed.

" There is not a woman in the two worlds of Ireland whom I have not brought before our son, and if among them all he cannot content himself it is because he cannot be contented."

" Now," said Fergne, " we are listening to the truth."

" Still," Boann insisted, "the child is sick."

" Make a suggestion," said the Dagda.

But she could not make a suggestion.

Also at that time she became ill at ease, and was agitated by movements and jerks, and half-sittings up and half-sittings down, so that even the Dagda noticed it.

" Dove of Time and Heart of the Heart of the World," said the Dagda, " tell me what it is that moves you and agitates you, so that you can neither sit nor stand nor stay easy? "

" I have seen too many women," Boann replied, " and I must go to some place where I can get the sight of them out of my eyes."

84

"Surely——" Fergne began in a tone of astonishment and expostulation.

"I wish," said Boann, "to go among my men-servants, and to watch them as they move with agility and circumspection about their work. I wish to look at our soldiers as they perform martial evolutions and leap and run. I wish to see short hair on heads and long hair on chins. I wish to see bald people——"

"Here," stammered Fergne, "is a wish indeed!"

"I wish to look into the eyes of oxen that do not squint or languish or peep. I wish to see legs," said she; "so I shall look steadily on horses and hens, on goats and sheep and warriors."

"In the matter of legs," said Fergne eagerly, "I can assure you——"

"I wish to look," she continued, "on hard and angular and uncomfortable things, for my mind is clouded and there is a bad taste in my mouth from the sight of those endless females."

"There is nothing," cried Fergne, "there is nothing more tonic to the soul or more lifting to the imagination——"

85

" I can quite understand," said Boann,
" why Angus would not lay a finger or an
eye on any one of them, for women are
hideous and hairy and ridiculous."

" This is not wisdom," said Fergne; " this
is not sound common sense."

" And," she continued, " when they are
not long and bony and unpleasant they are
short and stumpy and squashy, and I must
go away now until I can forget that there are
any of them living, and until I can discover
if there are truly men moving in the
world, for I have come to doubt all good
things."

Boann left them then, in a condition of
agitation and wrath, but Fergne thought that
he would shortly have two patients under his
hand, and that of the two it was the mother
who was the most rankly ill.

CHAPTER XXVII

" Now," said the Dagda, " I don't know
what to do, for I have shown Angus all the
women of the worlds, and, unless it was a

dream my son had instead of a vision, there
is a woman somewhere whom we have not
seen."

" That," Fergne commented, " is a ripe
statement of the case.   There must be some
one who has hidden a notable pearl, or there
is a dove that is modestly concealing itself
among the branches."

" Have you a suggestion to make? " said
the Dagda.

" I have."

" Then make it."

" Not hard to do," said Fergne, " and
here it is.   One of your vassal kings is
famous for his knowledge of visions and
apparitions and sorceries."

" Which of them is that? "

" It is Bove the Red, King over the Shí
of the Men of Femen, and if you set him on
the work he will discover the charmer that
we lack."

" Let a message be sent to that Shí," the
Dagda commanded, " to say that we will
ourselves follow the messenger and that we
shall expect a reply to our question."

" It may be," Fergne continued, " that
Bove will have to call up those visions again,

87

so I will go to him myself, for I should not like to miss the sight."

He set out then, and, when a reasonable time had elapsed, the Dagda followed with Angus, and they came to the Shí that Bove reigned over in Munster.

They were brought with all observance to the palace, and were given a feast which lasted for three days, and after the feast a banquet was given in their honour.

CHAPTER XXVIII

DURING the banquet a mood of depression came upon the Dagda, and, although Bove had every entertainment for him that was possible, the depression of the god deepened so that he could not listen to the people about him with calmness.

" Good my soul," said Bove in despair, " this banquet is in your honour."

" I cannot help that," the Dagda replied. " My mind is troubled and perplexed, and I feel a great inclination to weep."

" Weep then," Fergne counselled, " for

where there is a surplus of salt in the blood
weeping conveys away a quantity of that
surplus.   And," he continued, " it is because
women weep easier than men that they are,
on the whole, healthier than men."

" I feel," said the Dagda, " that the Heart
of the Heart of the World was right, and
that we have looked on too many women in
these visions, and I think that something
female and depressing comes on the mind
when it has been too extensively occupied
with that sex."

Fergne stared at the Lord of the Under-
world.

" You do not say that! " he gasped.

" My wife said it."

" I," Fergne asserted, " have never felt
better in my life than I feel now; and, by
my hand, if I could see those lovely visions
again, I should feel even better than I do
now.   For there is nothing more tonic to
the mind and more uplifting to the understanding than the vision of doves that abound
in health and beauty."

" Let it be so," said the Dagda in a tone of
resignation.

Bove wished to keep the Dagda in discussion, for by thus holding his mind he might withdraw it from the abyss of dejection into which it threatened to plunge.

" But," he cried to Fergne, " do you truly consider that salt is bad for the system? "

" As everything in excess is, as everything retained too long is, for we must get rid of all that we have or suffer from the retention. And whether it be salt or treasure that we amass we keep them at our peril, for, being kept, they rot and will breed a plague in either the body or the soul."

" But about this salt," Bove insisted, " what do you recommend us to do? "

" Let us do in this, and in all other cases, exactly what the ladies do. Let us weep," said Fergne.

" Let us weep," Bove echoed dismally.

" Let every man weep once a day," Fergne continued, " and in the morning for preference: he will thus cleanse his mind, and he will wash his eyes also."

" I should not know how to weep now," said Bove regretfully. " I have long forgotten how it is done."

" It is for such emergencies that physicians

are required," said Fergne, " and I shall tell you how to weep."

" Let us have that prescription," cried the Dagda.

" In the morning," Fergne commanded, " procure for yourself an onion; hold this close to your face and cut it with a blunt weapon, and in that way you will weep."

" And then I shall become as healthy as a woman," said Bove.

" Nearly so, but not quite," Fergne amended, " for the health of a woman truly depends on the amount of affection that she receives from a man. All women in love are healthy."

" I shall certainly search for an onion and an affectionate man," Bove commented.

But at that point the Dagda commenced to laugh.

At a sign from Bove a mether of wine was brought, and it was in extent like a well-sized field, and in depth it resembled a mountain pool, and the scent that came from it was like the fragrance of a clover meadow when the sun shines after rain.

The Dagda bent over this wine, and he gurgled into it so happily that the liquor foamed and creamed against the sides, and a thousand bubbles danced over the brim.

" Indeed, my good heart," said he, " you have made me weep, and my tears are salty."

" Do not taste them," commanded Fergne. " Do not re-imbibe that which you are counselled to reject."

" So far," said Bove, who wished to keep the Dagda occupied, " so far we have received excellent advice, and we may have weeping matches at fairs and tournaments; twelve men to weep against twelve women, and the winner to be presented with an onion. But I am in need of further advice."

" You are laughing at me," said Fergne, " and, as he who laughs will weep, you shall fulfil my prescription. I do not mind your laughter, however, and I am always ready to give advice to those who desire it."

" Nay," replied Bove, " this time it is the advice of our master that I seek."

" Tell me your perplexity, my love," said the Dagda.

CHAPTER XXIX

SAID BOVE:

Once there was a man in my service named Friuc. He had a wonderful art in the fattening of swine, but he was wonderful in everything that had to do with swine.

No person could make a pig go where he wanted it to go so willingly as Friuc could.

Everybody who knows anything knows that a pig would rather run a mile in the direction chosen by himself than sidle an inch along the track counselled by another: for pigs have unlimited confidence in themselves, but they have no faith in other creatures, nor have they any trust in the gods.

But Friuc could do whatever he pleased with a pig. They used to rub against his leg like pet dogs, and they always wanted to go to sleep with their heads in his lap. But, if they loved Friuc, Friuc loved them.

He might be impatient with a member of his family—he was never impatient with a pig. He might exclaim angrily against a horse that trod on his foot, but he would have

93

let a pig eat him.   However, although a pig
will eat anything, there was not a pork in
Munster that would lay a tooth on Friuc
otherwise than in affection.

On account of his mastery over, and his
understanding of pigs, Friuc was appointed
my Chief Swineherd.

It happened that the King of one of the
Western Shís, Ochall Oichni by name, had
a noted swineherd, one Rucht, and, unless
it was Friuc, this Rucht of Connacht had no
equal in swine tending.   He was a wonder.
These two were the champion pig tenders of
the Shí.   There were some who said that
Friuc was the better man of the two, but as
many held this to be inexact and claimed
that it was Rucht who took the branch.   But
these famous swineherds were great friends,
and they used to meet frequently to discuss
curious points about pigs.

Whenever there was a great fall of mast
in Munster Friuc would send news of it to
Connacht, and Rucht would come, playing
on a pipe, leading his charges behind him
to fatten in the good Munster beechwoods.

Friuc did this because he liked Rucht,
but more he did it because he could not bear

94

to think that any pig was going without his share of what was good for him.

On the other hand, when mast was plentiful in Connacht (which was not so often) Rucht would invite Friuc and his droves to the western forests, and they would go there galloping and would eat Connacht mast and grunt with delight and gratitude.

But the baser sort strove to arouse ill-feeling between the friends; for there are people who cannot bear to see friendship anywhere; people whose hearts are set in ill-humour and violence and war, and these people succeeded at last in raising bitterness between the swineherds.

CHAPTER XXX

There had been a great fall of mast in Munster.

Within the memory of man there had not been such a provision of the succulent nuts. Under the beech trees the ground was a foot thick in mast; and in places, deep in the forest, where growth was thick or the sun had ingress, the ground was covered to a depth of three feet with mast. And in yet other nooks and crannies of the loopy wood, where there had been a driftage caused by the wind, there were depressions of great profundity, and in these there was a choke and overflow of mast.

The swine of Munster, every pig of the Munster pigs, as well as those of the King, were led into, or let into, the forest by Friuc; and while they were there the sound that arose from among the trees became so deafening that all Munster thrilled to it, and no other sound was heard in the kingdom.

When one listened from a distance it seemed as if a violent sea and a storm of thunder were hammering against a circular rocky shore and echoing back and forth in mighty peals and clashings.

People who lived nigh the forest went mad from the exuberance of that uproar, and, under the delusion that they were swine, they bolted into the forest and pigged it among the pigs.

Those who lived farther away deserted their dwellings and sought hospitality afar.

And those who resided at yet greater

distances put plugs of hay into their ears and were enabled to exist in an uproar which they came to look upon as silence.

By day and night that noise, which was composed of squeals and screams; of grunts and gasps; of loud, nosey whistles and deep thrilling gurglings, continued; so that at last the only contented creatures in Munster were the pigs, and Friuc.

He moved tranquilly among his friends, looking at this one's muzzle and at that one's hoof; binding the torn ear of this innocent, and examining that bonneen which was still at milk and thriving on it.

He was happy, and he sent a messenger to Rucht to tell of the good fortune, and to invite him with his droves to the fête.

Rucht came, playing a rustic sweet air upon a pipe, and the swine of Connacht moved behind him in mighty concentrations.

Line after line, along a line that ran out of sight on either side, they came, and on the tails of the first line the noses of the second line rested.

And, behind them, farther than a crow's eye can peer, the pigs of Connacht galloped and pranced; sneezing because of the dust

they were raising; yawning after their beloved master, and at intervals making each
one the kind of noise with which he was
individually gifted.

They marched into the Beech Forests of
Munster and disappeared there. But if
they vanished from the eye the ear lost
nothing of them.

CHAPTER XXXI

BEFORE the Connacht swine arrived there
had been a brain-destroying uproar; but now
there was a noise for which no description
may be found.

Plugs of hay were no longer of any
use.

The ear-drums of people blew up inside
their heads and exploded violently into the
eye or the nose of the neighbour.

While those whose ears were tough took
to their heels and ran:

Pell-mell, hodge-podge, helter-skelter—

Charging into choked roads and unchok-
ing these by sheer impetus, and not a stop

did a man of them make until they came into Leinster of the Learned Men.

From there some surged sideways and westward to Connacht, while others fled to the north and the grim keeps of Ulster.

It was a marvellous time, a wild time, a time of madness. There were people who shouted:

" Death to the swineherds! "

And others who roared:

" Destruction to the pigs! "

Woe followed them, so that when a man went into a house and saw a piece of pork hanging from a rafter, he would go backwards out of the house with a buzz, and would not stop running until his wind gave out.

Or if a man saw a head of cabbage growing in a field it would remind him irresistibly of a slice of bacon, and he would leap on the cabbage with both feet until the last trace of anything but destruction vanished from the murdered plant.

So far for that.

Friuc and Rucht were where they liked to be—they were among pigs.

The noise of pigs was not a noise to

them.   It was a suitability, a thing worth listening to.

Nor did it silence them; for they were aware of the infinite gradation of sounds that is in all sound, and into these intervals of quietude, that were less noisy than the crash of Doom and only a little noisier than a hurricane, they injected such remarks as they wished to exchange, and felicitated each other on the happiness about them.

Thus the first day passed, and at night Friuc and Rucht lay down to sleep on the back of six large swine who were lying all in and out, and who had eaten so solidly that they could not wag a hoof, a bristle, or an ear.

Good sleep was with the comrades, and they rested till the dawn.

CHAPTER XXXII

I⊤ was the pigs they were lying on that awakened them, and although the language of swine is not comprehended by everybody, Friuc and Rucht understood it well.

This is what the pigs said:

" Darlings of all Darlings, and Pets of the Pigs of the World, get off our backs, for our food is digested, and there is more of it to be eaten."

They then, with precaution, rolled their masters to the ground, and they became jaws and enjoyment and a new portion of the contemporary noise.

Now it is a curious thing that women awaken in the morning uncomely but gay, while men arise to the new day as though they were being reborn into unhappiness; for at the dawn a man is ill-tempered, and a great discoverer of insult.

Friuc and Rucht, being males, were thus constituted. They arose with quietly bad tempers, and each did his best to look at a place where the other was not.

Also, they had no breakfast, for they had forgotten to bring any; and that lack assisted their uncheerfulness to become morose.

Rucht, as the visitor, considered that Friuc, as the host, should have provided him with food; and Friuc thought that the man who had come on a journey should have had the common prudence to bring food with him.

But the Connacht man did not quite see

his way to open a subject which must exacerbate his host, and a Munster man is too polite to refer to a personal grievance until he has transformed it into something else.

"They say in Connacht," Rucht commenced, "that you are a better swineherd than I am."

"And they tell me here in Munster," Friuc replied, "that it is you are the better."

"They are trying to make trouble between us," said Rucht with a sigh. "But they can't do it."

"That is true," Friuc agreed dolefully. "They are trying to make us fall out and we won't please them. But," he continued after a moment's pause, and in a deep and thoughtful voice, "But all the same——"

"All the same, what?"

"Nothing; I was thinking."

"I don't like these 'all-the-sames,'" commented Rucht.

"No one said you did," Friuc retorted.

"What are you driving at?" Rucht demanded hotly.

"I am driving at the thing the Connacht man hit when he aimed at the bird—nothing at all."

"All the same!" Rucht quoted morosely.

"Well, if you want to know what I was thinking, I'll tell you. I was thinking that the people who say I am the best swineherd are right, even if they are Connacht men."

"I was thinking the same thing," said Rucht, "but I was thinking it the other way round."

"I'll prove that I'm right," said Friuc.

"Prove it," his companion roared.

"Your pigs are here," Friuc continued, "and they can stay here, but not one inch of fat will one Connacht pig add to his Connacht ribs for all he eats; and the dear knows that a Connacht pig can eat nearly as much as a Connacht man."

And that happened, for Friuc put a spell on the foreign pigs.

The more they ate the thinner they got.

It was as though they were eating hunger, while the swine of Munster throve exceedingly.

Each of the Munster pigs had at first three chins to his jaw, but after a time they got six chins apiece. In another while they had chins all the way down to their hooves. Their stomachs fattened and descended until

103

they rested on the ground so that they had to go to sleep standing up.

Their eyes were so bolstered in fat that they could only look straight in front of them, and their tails disappeared in the overlapping rotundity of their hams.

CHAPTER XXXIII

BUT in the matter of the Connacht pig—

The more he ate the leaner he got.

He had been jowled like a Leinster bard, and chinned like a king's baby; but his chins tumbled off him two at a time, and his swagging jowl ran up into his ear.

He became gaunt as a winter wolf and spiny as a hedgehog.

His skull stuck out, lean as a hatchet and pointed as a spear.

His legs grew as lanky as a young foal's, and his upper anatomy was all chest and no stomach like a coursing hound.

His tail poked outwards and downwards like a piece of wet string pasted on a bone.

There was no curl in his tail.

Thus he was, and thus they all were.

As they grew skinny they became afflicted with a rage of eating which was terrifying, and with an agility to baffle the eye that watched them.

You could see what they did, but not how they did it, for they moved too fast.

They leaped into a place where mast was, scooped it clean in an hundred swift gobbles, and bounded thence to another place, with the bound of a red deer and the savagery of a bear.

Their hunger was such that they screamed from the rage of it, and the air whistled through their long lean snouts like the whistle of a wintry gale through a hole.

There were no people left in Munster but the deaf men, and they recovered their hearing; that is, they had hearing thrust violently upon them, and they cursed the gift as they fled.

The people far away in Leinster took to plugging their ears with wads of hay when they wanted to go asleep, but not a wink did they get.

The crows, who for a long time tried to

compete with the pigs, caved in, and gave up, and emigrated.

There wasn't a bird left in a tree, nor a beast left in a cave.

The worms of Munster went far underground, and maybe they perished there.

And the fish in the streams and rivers battered their noses to bits and broke their fins trying to swim up-stream against time.

They came floating back again with their bellies turned up, and not a wag left in a fin; dead they were.

It began to rain, too, for the noise brought the rain down.

But the Connacht pigs did not stop. They gave a squeal, a leap, a whistle, and a gobble, and they did that, all day long and all night long, as long as the mast lasted.

The mast could not outlast that ravage.

They cleaned the forests of mast in a day and a half.

They ate the leaves that had fallen.

They chewed the bark off the trees; at first as high as they could reach, but afterwards as high as they could jump; and they could jump like cats.

They rooted up the grass and ate it.

106

They ate clay.

They cleared the forests of all the droppings of all the pigs.

They picked up stones in their mouths, and mumbled at them until they got the toothache.

And they overturned Munster hogs that were too fat to right themselves, and ate the hooves off these while they lay helpless.

They would have eaten the young ones, only that Friuc stopped them, for he couldn't stand it.

" Be off with your pigs," he commanded. " Take them out of my forests and out of my sight, and don't let a hoof of theirs or of yours step in this land again."

" I'll go," Rucht replied, " but I know what you did and how you did it.

" I can do it myself," said he.

" You can crow here," he shouted, " but come to Connacht and crow if you dare.

" I'll do as much to your pigs as you did to mine, You-This-And-That of Munster! " he roared.

" Emigrate from here," cried Friuc; " get out of Munster," he cried.

" I will," Rucht replied, " I'll fly the land

where a man doesn't get his breakfast, and the pigs eat wind."

"Come on with you," he called then to his swine.

They ran howling, weeping, squealing to him, and he set himself at their head and started running like a hare.

CHAPTER XXXIV

He did not stop running until he got to Connacht, but the track of land that stretches from the Beech Woods of Munster to the Swine Pens of Connacht was a desert for years after their passing, for the Connacht pigs ate that land to the butt, and ruined it.

Friuc then took up Rucht's challenge and followed him with his swine.

But in Connacht the tables were turned on him, and the Munster swine became so lean that you could only see them by looking at them very steadily, and for a long time, and sideways at that; and, even then, it was only a streak you saw.

That was how enmity began between the

108

swineherds. The pigs of both were ruined, so that I told Friuc I did not want him any longer as a swineherd, and Ochall Oichni said the same thing to Rucht.

But the swineherds were unrepentant.

They did not want employment.

They had more than enough to do chasing each other, for that became their employment, and they went at it day and night.

Wherever they met they fought, and although each stretched the other at the door of death, neither of them was able to push the other through.

They began to change shapes then, thinking that in another form they might have a better chance; but they were always equal. One bit and the other tore, and the tear was as bad as the bite. They harried each other out of this shape and into that. They fought as birds, and in that shape they were known as Talon and Wing. Then they fought as sea-beasts and were called Shark and Whale. Then they became spectres called Shadow and Woe, and after that they were dragons. And in all these shapes they fought savagely.

Each of them half-killed and three-quarter killed his rival; but neither could absolutely get the victory over the other, and they cannot rest until they find out which of them is the better man.

They have been like that for seven years.

"What are they now?" the Dagda inquired.

"They are bulls, and they are both in Connacht in strong well-separated pens. They are in the Shí of Ethal Anbual, and they have been quiet for a long time."

"And what was the advice you wanted?" Fergne asked.

"I wanted to know how these enemies might be made friends again."

"They fell out over pigs, let them fall in over pigs. Feed them on bacon," said Fergne.

"They are not really enemies," said the Dagda. "They only wish to know which is the better man. It is not a question of hate, but of fact, that is between them, and when they have settled this they will be able to be friends again. But as they have taken up the burden of proof they must carry it through, and no one can help them."

Bove was contented with this statement, not because he was assisted by it, but because he noticed that the Dagda had forgotten his depression; and it was to make his master merry that he had told the tale.

Musicians and dancers and jugglers were then called in, and the gaiety of the Dagda was such that he gave rich presents to these entertainers, and, when the company separated for the night, each went to his bed in high good humour, but the Dagda went to sleep in the merriest humour of them all.

CHAPTER XXXV

On the day following the banquet the Dagda asked an account from Bove of the work he had ordered him to do.

" That girl," said he, " who has been destroying my son Angus; what have you discovered about her? "

" I have found the girl," said Bove.

" Was I a good counsellor? " Fergne cried joyfully.

" Who is she? " the Dagda inquired.

" She is Caer, the daughter of Ethal
Anbual, King of the Shí of Uaman in the
kingdom of Connacht; and she is in her
father's Shí at the Lake of the Dragon's
Mouth, hard by the place known as the Harp
of Cliach."

" Now," said Fergne, " Angus can go to
that place and take his treasure."

" I have no power," cried the mac an Óg
peevishly. " I am consumed by desire, and
cannot control my will."

" But let us be certain," the physician continued, " that you have found the right girl,
for if we make a mistake now we might give
the matter up in despair. Call her up in a
vision," he suggested eagerly.

So that was done.

The Dagda made first a darkness, and
then a golden radiance, and then they looked
through the purple haze which was beyond
the radiance.

They saw a sandy strip, and sunshine, and
a rolling sea: and upon that strand a band of
girls were romping. Among them there was
one taller than the rest, and, although the
others were beautiful, this one was so lovely
that she could scarcely be looked at. She

dazzled the eye as the sun does, and she filled
the mind with delight and wonder, so that the
person who looked at her forgot to think, and
could remember nothing beyond that beauty.

" Do you cry Hola to that? " gasped
Fergne. " If you do not say Hola to her
I shall say it myself."

" She is my love beyond the loves of the
worlds," said Angus, " she is the crown of
the soul and the fulfilment of desire."

" She is," cried Fergne. " I swear by
my hand that she is all that has been said, and
all that has not been said, and it is to her I
give the palm."

The vision then faded, and Angus sat with
Bove and Fergne on his either hand, and
they were all stupefied with wonder.

CHAPTER XXXVI

" WHY has Ethal Anbual concealed his
daughter from me? " the Dagda asked.

" He conceives that you have no right to
demand her," Bove replied.

" And it is true that I have no such right,"

said the Dagda, " and, therefore, there is no more to be said on this matter, and we may all go home."

" But the boy! " said Fergne, " the boy will fade away."

" Have you a suggestion to make? " said the Dagda.

" I have one," Bove interposed.

" Make it," said the Dagda.

" It would be very wrong of us to do a thing that was wrong," said Bove, " and, therefore, we shall not do it."

" We certainly shall not," Fergne agreed.

" But there are other people, and it is right for those people to do what is wrong."

" How so ? " said Fergne, scandalised.

" Wrongdoing is their base of existence," said Bove.

" What people are those? " the Dagda inquired.

" Mortals," Bove replied.

" Indeed," cried Fergne, " I do not often hear truth and wisdom spoken, but this time I hear it with my two ears."

" Give power for a day to mortals," Bove counselled. " They will get the girl for us, and there will be an end to all this anxiety."

"Who is the mortal King of Connacht?" the Dagda asked.

"There is not really a King," Bove replied; "there is a Queen and her consort."

"And this Queen?"

"She is Maeve, daughter of the High King of Ireland: she is the noblest of the queens of the world, and she is the most beautiful woman under the sun."

"I shall certainly look closely on that Queen," said Fergne.

"We shall visit Maeve of Connacht about the Feast of Samhain," said the Dagda, "for at that time the doors are opened between this world and that one, and whoever dares . . . Will this Queen dare to enter Faery?"

Bove replied to that with conviction:

"There is nothing that Maeve of Connacht would not dare, for she is not alone beautiful, she is greatly courageous."

"I shall seek her assistance," the Dagda announced.

"Now, Angus, my heart," cried Fergne jovially, "you may begin to get well, for although that fawn is not yet in your arms, she is condemned to them and cannot escape."

" I do feel better," said Angus; " I begin indeed to feel well."

" But," Fergne concluded, " the person I wish to see, and the person whom I must see, is this courageous and lovely Queen, for I feel assured that she is the Silk of the Flock and the Early Fragrance of the Hawthorn. How does this fawn look? " he asked. " Is she dark and slender and of a middle stature? "

" She is tall and well-rounded," Bove replied. " She is long-faced and pale, and her hair shines like gold."

" It is thus she should be," Fergne agreed, " and it is in that fashion I shall think of her."

CHAPTER XXXVII

THE Feast of Samhain was at hand, and when it wanted but three days to the Feast, the Dagda, with Angus and Bove and Fergne, set out for Connacht, and a company of sixty chariots went with them. They reached Connacht at noon of the day before the feast, and a messenger was sent from them to the palace demanding an interview with Ethal Anbual.

But the King of the Shí of Connacht refused to grant it.

" I know what the Dagda wants," he said; " I will not consent to give my daughter to Angus Óg."

When the messenger returned evening was advanced, and the hour was almost at hand when the doors are down between the two realms, so that the Dagda and his company mounted their chariots and drove in the direction of the door in the hillside. When they reached it the door was open, and they passed through it and rode into the world of men.

From the hillside to the palace at Cruachan Ai was but a short journey, and in five minutes the guards at Cruachan reported that a company was advancing on the palace. In another minute preparations had been made to receive them, and in one minute more they were at the fortifications.

They were ushered into the palace with ceremony and respect, for neither the guards, the chamberlains, nor the servants had ever before seen a host so beautifully apparelled,

117

or with such comely dignity of bearing, for they were plumed and crested with fire, and they were radiant as the sun itself.

Maeve was seated on her throne in the great reception hall, but when the Dagda appeared so great was his majesty and so noble his regard that she rose to receive him, and seated him on a throne beside her own, so that the Dagda sat on her right hand, Ailill, her husband, on her left, and the other people of the Shí were given honourable places.

" Will you tell your name and qualities yourself," asked Maeve, " or shall we send for your heralds to recite them? "

" I am the Dagda Mór," said her guest. " I am the High King of the people of Dana, and Lord Supreme of the Kingdoms of the Dead."

" And I am Maeve of Cruachan, daughter of the High King of Ireland, and Ruler of the Realm of Connacht."

The people of the Dagda and Maeve's people were introduced to each other in seemly order, and then, for Maeve was a famous housekeeper, a feast was brought in, and for the space of three hours it was enjoyed by all who were present and was praised.

CHAPTER XXXVIII

" I THINK," said Fergne, who had been looking at Maeve as one in a trance, " I certainly
think that this Queen is more worthy to be
called Hola to than even the daughter of
Ethal Anbual is."

" This Queen is married," Bove remarked.

" Would you limit the joy of life? " cried
Fergne reproachfully. " Would you put a
stay to happiness? "

He stroked the beard that flowed down to
his middle like a river of silver silk, and
became lost in that contemplation.

The Dagda then set before Maeve the
whole of the story that has been told, and,
after she had spoken with her counsellors,
and been advised by them that she should
have nothing to do with the matter, Maeve
decided that she would give the assistance
required.

" For," said she, " I have never yet paid
a visit to Faery, and as I am the ruler of
Connacht I should like to see the ruler of the
Shí of my own country."

One of her counsellors interposed:

" There has always been peace between the Shí and Cruachan; but after this there may be ill-feeling and bicker, and who knows if the High King of the Shí will protect us from the vengeance of the Tribes of Dana."

" I will answer for that," replied the Dagda. " No harm shall come to Connacht from the people of the Shí, although much may happen in Connacht in consequence, for no action can cease until it has worked out all its possibilities."

" If you guarantee me against the Shí," said Maeve, " I will be my own guarantor for all that may happen in Connacht or in Ireland."

That was settled, and, as the evening was advanced and the darkness great, it was decided that they should set out at once while the doors of Faery were open, and in half an hour Maeve, at the head of a thousand chariots, was dashing to the hill of Cruachan.

CHAPTER XXXIX

SHE sacked the Shí of Uaman, and took away booty and treasure, and she took Ethal Anbual and all his chief people prisoner, and she brought away from the Shí two young bulls, one of which was known as The White-horn and the other was called The Brown Bull.

" These bulls," said Ethal Anbual, as he stared fiercely on Maeve, " will avenge me."

" They will do what they can," Maeve replied, " and in order that you may have a fair chance of being revenged, I shall keep the bulls."

" That is sound sense and queenliness," said Fergne.

" And," said Bove, " our famous Swine-herds are off on their travels again."

" Are those the two you told me of? " the Dagda inquired.

" They are the identical two," Bove answered. " There go Friuc and Rucht."

" There is many a man of Ireland and of Connacht will come to my realm because of these bulls," Ethal Anbual repeated.

121

" Is that true? " Maeve inquired.

" It is not a lie indeed," the Dagda replied.

" We must all come sometime to the Country of the Dead," said Maeve, " and whether we come on account of these bulls or on some other account does not greatly matter, and, therefore, I shall take the bulls."

" And now about your daughter! " said the Dagda.

" My daughter is no concern of yours," replied Ethal Anbual.   " It is true that I am your vassal, and in all proper ways I render obedience and service, but my daughter does not come within your rights."

" That is verity," the Dagda agreed.   " I do not properly see what we can do."

" I do not wish to see my daughter married to the mac an Óg," Ethal Anbual continued, " for there is a feud between Angus and myself, and therefore I shall not give her up to him."

" There is nothing left us but to go home," said the Dagda.

" But we cannot go home until we have performed what we set out to do," Bove insisted.

" Have you a suggestion to make? " cried the Dagda.

" I have indeed."

" Then make it," said the Dagda.

" It is," said Bove, " that if this thing is to be done by mortals, we should let mortals do it."

" Now . . ." cried Fergne.

But Maeve broke in tempestuously:

" I came to get this girl, and I shall not go away until I have got her."

" I think also," she continued, turning fiercely on Ethal Anbual, " that it is an impertinence for any chit to refuse the embraces of a proper man like Angus."

" The girl does not wish for these embraces," he replied stubbornly.

" Let her wish or not wish, she must be given to me, for by my hand, I shall not leave without her, and the booty I have already seized is nothing to the plunder I shall presently take unless that girl is given to me."

" That is the way to talk," cried Fergne. " It is thus deeds are done, even by a dove."

" The girl does not desire to go," said Ethal Anbual. " I cannot force her. She is a Mistress of Arts."

123

" How do you know that she does not wish to go with Angus? " asked the Dagda.

" She told me that herself," he replied triumphantly.

" That settles it," said the Dagda mournfully. " If she does not wish to go she cannot be forced."

" Of course she wishes to go," cried Maeve.

" But she told her father . . ."

" What a girl tells her father is seldom of any importance and is never true."

" She is cold-headed as a spring morning," cried Fergne. " She is warm-blooded as a summer noon. Now we are listening to wisdom indeed."

Maeve leaned to Ailill.

" That companion of the Dagda pleases me very much, and although he is old he is robust."

She turned again to Ethal Anbual.

" If you wished to conceal your daughter, why did you send her wraith and vision to Angus the mac an Óg? "

" By my word," cried Ethal Anbual, " I did not send that vision, and, by my hand, I would not let the son of the Dagda see anything I possess, for he is envious, and a thief."

" If you did not send the vision," said Bove, " who sent it? "

" I know nothing of that."

" The girl sent it herself," said Maeve, " and she sent it because she wanted Angus to see her, and to desire her, and to come after her."

" Yes? " said Bove.

" And the reason she wanted the mac an Óg to desire her was because she desired the mac an Óg."

" This Queen gets the palm," cried Fergne. " I cry Hola to this Queen, for she is the Pulse of the Heart, and the very Tongue Tip of Wisdom."

" That nobleman," said Maeve to Ailill, " is not only pleasant and courteous and robust; he is also intelligent."

" Where is this girl? " she demanded of Ethal Anbual.

" She is at the Lake of the Dragon's Mouth," he replied sullenly.

" Go there," Maeve counselled to Angus Óg. " You will find that she is waiting for you, and you will find that she is impatient."

" And now," she said, turning to Ethal
Anbual, " I shall return the booty I took
from you; that is, the Crown of Bruin, the
Mantle of Laery and the Shirt of Dunlaing,
for I did not come to sack the Shí, but to
give help to the Dagda, and to bring two
lovers together."

" You will also return The Whitehorn and
The Brown Bull," said Ethal Anbual.

" I shall not give them back," she cried.
" You have threatened me about those bulls,
and against a threat I will maintain my
defiance and my power.

" And now," said she, " I will go back to
my own country."

The Dagda then gave her three kisses, and
it was thus Maeve of Cruachan went into
and out of Faery on that occasion.

CHAPTER XL

" THAT is the story of the sacking of the Shí
of Cruachan," she said to Fergus.

She turned to Nera.

" But next Samhain I shall go there again,

and I shall not leave what will be worth any king's reigning over."

" Tell me," said Fergus, " what happened to those bulls you took from the Shí? "

" The Whitehorn is here in Connacht. It is the master of my husband's herds, but The Brown Bull would not stay with us; it took itself away to Cuailgne in Ulster, and it is just as well that it did go off, for Connacht is not wide enough to hold two such bulls. No person could sleep for their roarings at and challengings to each other, and if they meet, one or both of them will be dead before they can be separated. Therefore, I do not greatly mourn for the loss of The Brown Bull. But as it is," said she, " there is not a bull in the whole of Connacht that dares to give one bellow out of him for dread and terror of The Whitehorn."

" And the threat of Ethal Anbual as to the disasters to be worked in Ireland by reason of those bulls? "

" That," said Maeve, " will be as it will be. But you do not drink! " she cried to Nera.

" I must crave your leave to depart before

127

the door in the hillside closes," said Nera, " for I made a bargain and a compact with my comrade that I would surely return to her."

" If you must return, you must return," Maeve replied, " and we will ourselves go with you a little distance, and will send with you our greetings and affection to that lovely lady you told us of."

" When you come next Samhain," said Nera, " you will not sack her house."

" We shall spare that house for your sake and for hers," the Queen answered.

Nera set out then with Maeve and a royal company, and when they reached the hillside he bade them farewell, and they bade him farewell with a blessing.

Then Maeve returned to Cruachan Ai with her people, and Nera went on into the Shí, and 'tis said that he will not come out of the Shí till Doom.

PART II

THE FEAST OF LUGNASA

CHAPTER I

" I," SAID Fergus mac Roy, " have had many adventures, but I have never taken part in the sacking of a Shí."

" It is an adventure that rarely occurs," said Ailill, comforting his guest.

" It is one," Maeve supplemented, " that seldom happens in Ulster."

Fergus stirred uneasily, for, although he had left Ulster in wrath, he yet loved tenderly his native province and one-time kingdom.

" Great and strange deeds have happened in Ulster," he replied.

" Surely," said Maeve. " It is surely so; and it is so that great and strange deeds have been done in every spot of Ireland. But the whole world knows how famous Connacht is for noble and wonderful happenings.

" It was Connacht that sacked a Shí of the World of the Gods," she continued. " It was not Leinster or Ulster or Munster that

did this deed.   It was my own kingdom—
this Connacht; and my own self — this
Maeve, your Queen, that did it.   And it
was Connacht again, and my own uncle, that
did it once before."

"When was it done before?" Fergus
demanded.

"My uncle, Eochaid [1] Airem, sacked the
Shí of Midir."

"I have heard much of Midir and of
Eochaid, but nothing of that sacking,"
Fergus commented.

"Ulster historians," said Maeve, "are
perhaps too busy escaping death by scant
victuals to care much for history."

"Let that be," said Fergus, "but I, who
reckon the gods in my kindred, am interested
in all that can be told about them."

"Well," said Maeve, "we, too, are of the
gods, and I can tell you somewhat of them."

"Let the Bell-Branch be rung," cried
Fergus.   "We must have this tale."

The Queen smiled tenderly on him, and
on his interest in her story-telling, while the
company set busily to their liquor, and then
turned expectantly to the Throne.

[1] Eochaid : pronounced Yóhee.

Said Maeve:

In the days that have passed, and that will not come again, Lugh of the Long Hand, Master of Arts and God of Gods,[1] presented the kingdoms of the Shí and of the earth to his son, Eochaid mac Elathán, called the Dagda Mór, the Great Good God, and it was the Dagda Mór who was King of the World and of the Underworld, until Angus Óg succeeded him.   The Dagda married Boann, the daughter of Delbaeth.   These two, the Dagda and Boann, were called the Two Young Ones, and the son of the Two Young Ones was Young Angus.   While the mac an Óg was a lad, the Dagda sent him in fosterage and tutelage to two lords of the Shí: one of these lords was Elcmar and the other was Midir, lord of the Shí of Bri Leith.   He was a prince of territory, a prince of wisdom, a prince of beauty; and his Shí was invested and conquered and sacked by my uncle, Eochaid Airem, High King of Ireland.

But that was in our time, while the time that I shall first tell of lies in dreadful distances of the past.

[1] London = the Dún of Lugh (pronounced Loo), seems to be named after this deity.

CHAPTER II

THE gods love women as women deserve to
be loved; and, therefore, this god had two
wives. The one was named Fuamnach and
the other was called Etain Echraide, Etain of
the Steeds.

Man or god is so constituted that he cannot equally do two things at a time, nor love
equally two things at a time; for he lives in
time and is ruled by it. Midir admired
Fuamnach; he was guided by her counsel:
but he loved Etain, and was more moved
by her whim than by the wisdom of her
partner.

So matters were when the mac an Óg, the
Treasure of Faery, and the Pride of the Great
Good God came to Shí Nenta of Bri Leith in
tutelage.

There is but one thing a man can love
easier and more faithfully and more deeply
than he loves a woman.

" Your pardon, Majesty," Fergus interposed, " but excepting for war there is no
such thing."

134

" It is a secret," said Maeve, " but there is one such thing. A man can love a man better than he loves a woman. That is, he can so love his son, his fosterling, or his scholar."

" It is true," said Ailill, turning on the stripling, his fosterling and charioteer, whose bright eyes were heavy with sleep, and who was only awake by courtesy.

" It is so," mourned Fergus, thinking deeply of the absent Cuchulinn.

He turned to Maeve.

" He could twist me about his middle finger. He is my heart's pet," he growled.

" Have I heard of this young man before?" said Maeve suspiciously.

" Connacht historians ——!" Fergus replied grimly. " He is one that will be heard of."

" An Ulsterman! "

" No," Fergus replied, a little embarrassed. " But," and he looked haughtily about the great room, " but for an Ulsterman I may suffice my company."

Maeve's eyes sparkled at and softened upon him.

" You are our delight," she said. " You are our treasure."

135

It is so that a man can love a man. And what a man, what a son, what a fosterling was Young Angus!

Beauty and courage, wisdom and gentlehood—these are his qualities. The sun and the air shine by his eye. The birds and the world sing by his lips. By his breath the flowers bloom; and all that is of health and colour and gaiety flows from his fingers.

Midir loved Fuamnach, and yet more he loved Etain; but more again, and yet more an hundredfold, he loved Angus the son of the Dagda Mór.

If it was easy for Midir to love Angus it was yet easier for Etain to love him, and it would not be hard for Fuamnach to love him either.

All these things happened.

CHAPTER III

ONE grows used to that to which one is accustomed, and Fuamnach was accustomed to the preference which her lord showed to Etain. That had become a daily and a nightly thing. It lay in the routine of life,

136

and the discontent that it had at first engendered had dulled, and been partly forgotten, and completely forgotten. Fuamnach could, or thought that she could, neglect her heart in the conduct of a king's household, and regain in usefulness that which she seemed to lose in love.

Then Angus came, and the world doted after him.

What now was Midir to Etain?

He was a name, a shadow, an importunity; a block that tripped her, and delayed her, and exasperated her. He was a sound that droned around her like a ghostly bagpipes, an expostulation that wailed about her very feet when they wished to move to a tryst with Angus.

" I do not quite understand," said Ailill. " How did the mac an Óg come to have this freedom with the King's wife? "

" It is perfectly right," said Maeve, " for it was Angus was the King, and Midir was his subject; and it has never yet been suggested that the rights of a supreme lord can be questioned in any household that is subject to him."

137

" It is certainly the law and the custom," said Ailill.

" All women know," Maeve continued, " that when a woman ceases to love her husband she may yet not come to hate him. She may love something else instead—her children, her gear, herself. But if, at that time, she falls in love with another man, then she can come to detest the husband who still adores her, and who cannot help doing so."

Here the great Queen's eye rested earnestly and serenely on Fergus mac Roy.

" For," she continued, " while a man is not lovable in unfaithfulness, a woman is still more lovable and desirable when she is unfaithful than when she is not."

" That could be queried," her husband interposed.

" By whom? "

" A woman never knows what a man thinks," Ailill replied, " for a man never tells the truth to a woman.   He couldn't."

" Ah! "

" Nor would a woman know what was said if she heard the truth."

" A   man's   thoughts   and   a   woman's

138

thoughts," said Maeve, " there is very little difference between them."

" Oh! " Fergus expostulated.

" There is no difference between them," said Maeve.

CHAPTER IV

WHEN Angus came, Fuamnach, who was young in body and sage in mind, grew younger again in both body and mind.   She sang; her eyes sparkled; and the tenderness that she felt for one alone was shown by her to every person in her palace, and to everything that was in her grounds.   She doted on cows and horses; she could have embraced her pigs and her hens; she looked tenderly on stones and trees;   as for her servants she became their sister.

For, as her husband did not desire her, and as the young lord would undoubtedly exercise his rights, she thought that it might be upon her the choice would fall; and that, falling so, it would be a harmless choice.

She imagined, as we imagine in dream, that she would know a happiness and a cherishing to which she was a stranger, and for which she yearned. And, of which too she had been frustrated, that she would herself actively cherish, and actively give happiness.

She had seen Angus, and her heart had gone to him as water flows down a hill: without effort, without thought. To this point the water comes, urging again a little, and still straining apace, and at this point it strives no more; it falls down and down, an eager, unconscious vertigo and abandon.

And it is so with love.

For love is unsought, it is unasked, it is incurious, and wills but to fall and fall, and to cease never from falling.

" If a person waited for these loves to happen——! " said Ailill, with a short laugh.

" That person would find them happening every spring," cried Maeve.

" Is love not eternal? " Fergus interrupted, scandalised.

" Have you found it so? " she answered.

" I . . ." said Fergus thoughtfully.

" Happy love is eternally renewed for those who are happy. Unhappy love is

eternally renewed for those who are not gay.
Is Connachúr gay? Are his love affairs
happy?"

"Even the gods are unhappy in love,"
Fergus replied.

The Queen's lovely face grew stern and her
deep male voice grew deeper.

"All beings are unhappy in love," said
she; "all love is unhappiness."

"It is perhaps unhappiness that men
love," quoth Ailill moodily.

"Love and war," Fergus murmured, "unhappiness and death, that is what men love."

"And food," said Maeve briskly; "men
do love food."

At this Fergus burst into joyous laughter,
and the Queen rung a peal with him.

"You are our treasure!" she said.

CHAPTER V

BUT there was no such happiness in store for
Fuamnach as that she dreamed of; for a
person who is born to ill-luck is born only to
ill-luck, as a thistle is born only to spikes.

She was in the young lord's path. He saw her, he spoke to her, he smiled upon her, as only he could smile or talk or look; and these three things, in the man who is their master, are an ecstasy and a bewilderment to the woman who seeks them, or finds them.

But, in a little, she saw that when the mac an Óg looked at her he did not see her. When he spoke to her he did not address her ; and when he smiled at her it was in absence of mind.

As one awakens, clear-eyed and shivering, on a bitter morn of winter, so she awakened. She saw that it was to Etain his eyes went ; it was to Etain he spoke, and at Etain that he smiled.

And she saw that Etain was rapt away, and sunk away, and drowned away and away in that look and smile and speech.

She saw that Etain's eyes had become diamonds drowned in dew.

That her mouth had become a rose drenched in dew.

That she had become all a meltingness and a flowing of milk and honey and spiced airs.

That she was suddenly one liquid

graciousness ; with a proud neck and an humbled shoulder; with timid ankles and a daring hand.

Fuamnach saw and her heart beat within her like a ram, and beat no more.   But her mind burned within her so fiercely that she must close her eyes lest strangers should see the flame of that furnace.   For, at a stroke, all else that lived became strangers to her, and there validly existed but Angus and Etain and herself.

Life and to spare was in that trio, and her heart of hate was universe enough for them all.

She was happy now, for who can exist without love, and hate is love.   Her day was filled with vision and her night with dream. She dreamed of Death in the day, and in the night she saw Death and Death and Death. She saw three Deaths, and their names were Etain and Angus and Fuamnach.   And she thought that with that swallowing the maw even of Death could be cloyed, and that he need eat no more.

CHAPTER VI

" A question here," said Ailill, " for I am not quite satisfied with the telling of this story."

" Ah——! " said Maeve haughtily.

" For my part," Fergus interrupted, " I think that this tale is excellently managed. It is perhaps told in a more manly fashion than is usual in love stories——"

" Or than is usual in a female narrator," Ailill supplemented.

" I am less of a female than you are," said Maeve. " I am a queen, and by that office I am a man——"

" I am a woman in my love affairs," she explained to Fergus, " but," and she turned again to Ailill, " in all that pertains to skill and hardihood and reason, I am a man."

" So! " said her husband. " But that is not my question. The lord Angus, Tanist of the Worlds, was at that time only a boy, and therefore he could not have aroused the dreadful passions that this story tells of; for love is shown to a child in kindnesses and playfulnesses, and not at all in vertigoes and abandonments and all these desperations that you tell of."

Maeve's mouth opened, but no word came, for she was nonplussed. "You—you could tell this story better!" she shrilled.

Ailill spread abroad hands of deprecation: "I," he began, "I am unpractised in story-telling——"

"Wait," said Fergus, "for it is only an Ulsterman can resolve this discrepancy, which would indeed be a blot on the tale if it were left unanswered."

"An Ulsterman?" said Maeve.

"As Angus Óg is."

"Oh!" said Maeve.

"For although Ulster historians may not know all that is to be known about the Shís of Connacht, they are yet not unlearned in the Shí-craft of their own land."

"Well!" said Maeve.

"Angus, when quite a boy, was sent in tutelage to the god Elcmair, the Dagda's brother-in-law, and it was with Elcmair that he remained until he was fitted for a nobler teaching. His education in magic and divination was to be completed by Bove of the Shí of the Men of Feman, my grandfather——"

" Your grandfather! " quoth Maeve.

" Yes," said Fergus, " my mother, Roy, was daughter to the Red of Faery, Bove of Shí Femen. I am of the gods on my mother's side, and it is thence that my name, Choicely-Unique, comes."

" You are our treasure," said Maeve earnestly.

Fergus continued:

" When the education of the lord Angus was completed by Bove the Red, he was sent for instruction in special magic to the lord Midir you speak of. Angus, therefore, was already a young man when he went to Shí Nenta of Bri Leith.[1]

" More," Fergus continued. " Angus fell in love with Elcmair's daughter Englic, but she was carried off in a raid made by my grandfather's three sons out of Shí Finda-brach; and 'tis said that Prince Midir of Shí Nenta was also in love with that dear lady. Neither he nor Angus, but one of my Faery uncles, got her."

" This is news to me," said Maeve.

" It follows that Elcmair's daughter was Angus Óg's first love, and that——"

---

[1] In the Other World, Bri Leith parallels the County Longford.

" Hold," cried Maeve indignantly.   " It is well known that Angus Óg's first love was my own sister Derbrenn.   Every cultivated person is aware that Derbrenn, daughter of Eochaid Feidleic, was Angus Óg's first love."

She appealed to her husband:

" You are from Leinster, and must have heard the story of the Six Swine from Faery."

Ailill nodded, and replied : " My Hospittaller's wife tried to cut a steak off the belly of one of them."

" Brogarban," said Maeve triumphantly.

She turned to Fergus again.

" While she was in Faery with Angus, my sister was the fosterer of six young people that visited the earth later on in the shape of boars so that they might find and eat the Food of the Gods, the Nuts of Knowledge. It is in Connacht, apparently, that the Food of the Gods is to be found, and it was I myself that prevented these beings from eating the nuts of my territory, and I myself killed five of them at the one hunting."

" Brogarban escaped," said Ailill.

He turned to Fergus.   " Brogarban was his name as a boar, but in the Shí his name is Flann.   He is there now."

" So you see," said Maeve, " that my
sister——"

" No," said Fergus decidedly, " your
sister, Derbrenn, may have been the mac an
Óg's first *earthly* love, but the tale that you
are telling goes back more than a thousand
years, and, therefore——"

" I am being bothered with interruptions,"
cried Maeve angrily. " One of the druids
can finish this story, if he is let."

" Oh no," Fergus soothed her. " It is
settled that at the time you speak of, Angus
Óg was of an age and dignity to exercise the
rights that are mentioned. Your case is
proved."

" You see," Maeve cried, turning triumphantly on her husband, " you see that I am
right again."

" You were certainly right," said Ailill
heartily, " and I beg that you continue the
story."

A thunder of applause came from the
audience, and Maeve bowed graciously and
delightedly to them, and intimated that the
drinking vessels of all should be filled before
the tale recommenced.

148

CHAPTER VII

THE tuition of Angus came to an end, and the time arrived for the young Master of Magic to return to his father's palace at the Brugh. He departed, but he did not go alone. Midir's wife, Etain, went with him, and Midir was left without the fosterling he adored, without the wife he loved, and with the wife that he did not care for.

This will happen to the man who has two wives; the wife of his heart will preserve him from the ill-humour of the wife of his house; for it is upon her the other's jealousy will be vented; and, in the feeling of triumph and satisfaction that she has, the bad temper of her rival can be taken as an importunate compliment.

But there was no love left in Midir's household. He did not love Fuamnach; and she did not love him. She loved Angus, or, perhaps, by sheer hate, she loved Etain.

A man or woman who do not love each other may live together in a tepid friendship that is not unhappy, creating duties and interests that absorb them and make life

149

palatable. But if he or she is torn by desire
that cannot be accomplished, then misery
comes, and that household grows to resemble
a den where cats scratch and screech, or a
cave where bears gloom and growl.

And those gods were frustrate!

Fuamnach, save for an instant of rage,
could not recall her mind from Angus; and
Midir, knowing that his foster-son was happy,
could not but remember Etain.

A love-tormented woman grows sick and
thin and angry. She looks like a wrinkled
apple, sour to the eye and the taste, and her
tongue is vinegar. The love-tormented man
grows heavy, grows dull, grows diligent in
doing nothing and in talking of many
nothings. Men fly him, for he is solemn
even in his drink; and women mock him,
for his eyes are lack-lustre, his hands are
slack and he walks like a clod.

So this household was, and such were
these poor gods.

Calamities such as these, and all calamities
whatever, react differently on a man and on
a woman. Energy is drained out of a man
in the presence of an evil that he is unable to
confront; but in the woman who is thus

assailed a demoniac energy is born; and she will not be at rest until the very ghost of hope is dead. Therefore, in desperate events and hopeless courses, the advice of a woman is more to be sought and is better worth following than anything a man can devise.

For men are reasonable, that is, they are timid; and when they are faced with defeat they will surrender; but women prefer their desire to any reason that can be imagined, and do not surrender while the ghost of a hope remains.

On the departure of Etain, Midir gave up hope. The deed was done, and an end was come not alone to her presence but even to the love that she had borne him. There was no future for that dead thing, and he addressed himself to the duties of his station and his kingdom.

A bleak peace was there for him, and he enjoyed it as his neighbour might enjoy a toothache.

CHAPTER VIII

BUT Fuamnach had not even that peace, and did not seek it.

She retired to her mind, and wove there, and destroyed there, web on web of plot, until her mind seemed to be the mesh of a vast spider, and she netted a whole world in it.

Anything is possible to the person who intends to do that thing and will abide the consequences; so, day by day, the intention of Fuamnach hardened and grew clear and grew urgent—and, day by day, the courage that is compacted will grow more and more certain of itself—and, which is a slower business, grew more and more eager for the deed.

There is the courage that is mere foolishness or obedience; the courage that is just energy or youthfulness; and the courage that comes of a matured intention, or the overcoming of fear; and this of them all is the courage to be dreaded, and the one that can scarcely fail.

Here Fergus interposed thoughtfully:
" I am neither young, nor foolish, nor

obedient, yet I should not think of myself as lacking in courage, nor would I go into combat otherwise than cheerfully."

" I also," said Ailill, " love life and do not fear death."

" It is still as I have said," Maeve replied, " for from the years of infancy a gentleman is trained to fight; is urged to fight; is told enthusiastically tales of fighting. Every vice is forgiven him if he will consent to fight; and thus, day by day, the intention to fight is formed in the boy's mind; so that fear is overcome at last, and he fights as by instinct."

" So! " Fergus pondered. " It is exactly so," he conceded.

The Queen continued:

It is not easy for a woman to overcome fear, for pain or even great exertion affrights her; but when she does overcome it, she is more fearless than any man can be. For a man may not be afraid to die, but he may be afraid to be dishonoured. He may not be afraid to be a rogue, he may be afraid not to be one when his fellows are. He may laugh at the law and its punishments, and may be afraid of the dark. There is a cowardly spot in every man, however courageous he may prove himself to be.

" I am not afraid of any of these things," said Fergus.

" You were afraid of breaking your geasa," said Maeve, " and by that fear you are an exile, and by that fear you let Deirdre and the sons of Uisneac die."

Fergus stared, and his face grew red as fire.

" Oh! " he said.

" And I," said Ailill, " where is my secret fear? "

" You are a good husband," the Queen replied, " and therefore you are afraid of your wife."

The company broke into great laughter, in which Ailill joined as heartily as any.

So a man can be a coward until he dies. But for the woman who has overcome fear there is no spot left of cowardice, except in the love she has for her children.

Fuamnach had no children. She was free to attempt any event that she pleased, and to be perfectly certain that she could accomplish it.

CHAPTER IX

THERE was a druid in Midir's household named Bresil Etarlaim. By the power of his will he could withdraw the wraiths of men from other places, or from other worlds; and he was as learned in guiles and stratagems as he was in wizardries.

A woman might guess at the bribe that Fuamnach offered, but we do not truly know how she suborned this magician to aid her against his lord, the King.

Between her and Bresil a plan was made; and, in accordance with this, she changed her manner of being.

She became thoughtful for and attentive to Midir.

He began to see that her eyes rested on him softly, and he could hear that her voice was as tender as her eyes.

Nor did these things displease him. If from the laxity of his mood she could not aim to be his comforter she could at least be his confidante; and in so delicate a matter how could he have another than she? His plaint of arid existence was uttered into her ears; and she gathered an hundredfold the tale of vanished perfections and memorial graces with which his mind was burthened.

She could give the sympathy of a commiserating hand on that bowed head, and words of murmured hope. It was mostly of hope that she spoke, for it is only in hopeless events that hope is an oracle and is remembered.

She took his hand in hers, soothing it, and she soothed his eyes with her own.

" Angus is young," she said, " and youth is inconstant. Etain is indeed the perfection you tell of, but what are perfections to a youth? Strange things and new things, these only are beautiful to the young."

But Midir shook his head in tragic unbelief.

" Even now," she urged, " Etain may seem to him not so beautiful as she was; and in a little she will not be beautiful at all. She may already be eclipsed by a woman who has straighter hair or curlier hair; or who has no hair at all; or one who is lovely because she has freckles; or amazing because she has two left legs."

156

But Midir shrugged that suggestion away.

" Indeed," Fuamnach insisted, " to a young man who has seen much of one woman every other woman seems more desirable, and he could adore her grandmother from sheer need of variety."

" It might be so with others," said Midir, " it could not be so with Etain."

" Believe, dear lord, that it could be so with anybody."

Midir waved unbelief and despair to her with a dying hand.

CHAPTER X

BUT, on the instant that was propitious, Fuamnach returned to her conversation, and Midir hurried to it also, for to talk about Etain had become his lacerating delight.

" More," said Fuamnach to his arid ear. " The mighty position of Angus renders him an easy prey for all who will to approach him. As the sun is seen by all, so he is seen by all. The world and the gods come to him; he sees all that is to be seen; and scarcely will

you find one who does not wish to be well
seen by Angus."

"And then!" said Midir.

"There will be a dimpling smile wherever he looks. A soft and bashful glance
wherever he looks. A wooing humbleness
wherever he looks."

Midir's breast rose as from a chasm:

"It would be so," he said.

"Ah! sweet lord, already it must be so.
It must be even now that Etain is sitting
alone; wondering, as in a cold dream, why
she should be solitary, or how that loneliness
can be."

"If it be thus . . .!"

"In how short a time will she come to
hate a loneliness that is seen by others even
more plainly than it is seen by herself?"

"So!" said Midir. "So! and what
follows?"

"That follows that must follow. She
will turn with eagerness, she will run with
delight to any person who will rescue her
from that too public solitude."

"So! So!" said Midir, with hurried
breath.

"And, if my lord is not at hand, she may

158

seek refuge in the arms of some one who is
not my dear lord."

" Oh! " cried the appalled Midir.

" It could be so! " she said.

" Yes," Fuamnach continued, looking
away in vastnesses of time and space and
surmise, " it could indeed be so; for there
is no other way that it could be, and our
darling may be doubly lost to us."

" And I——! " cried Midir, staring and
frantic.

" You are all gentleness, lord, as it is
right that power should be."

" Indeed, I am powerful," groaned the
god, " but in this event what can power or
powerlessness do? "

" Listen! " said Fuamnach.

And Midir, all ears and bated breath,
leaned to her tender eye.

" You can make it certain that Etain is or
is not lost."

" How so? "

" Or is not about to be lost."

" What shall I do? "

" Go to the Brugh.   Go to the palace of
the Dagda, where Angus is.   See the mac
an Óg, and discover what is in his heart.   I

shall see Etain, and will unlock all that is in hers.   Then we shall know."

" And with knowledge the heart can be at rest," said Midir deeply.

" So," said Fuamnach.

CHAPTER XI

THEY went to the Brugh of the Boyne and Bresil Etarlaim went with them.

They were admitted to the Dagda's palace, for how could they not be?   And how could there be another whom Angus more loved to see than his fosterer Midir? Or how could there be a happier man than Midir was, with his hand on the shoulder of his fosterling and his eyes looking into those dear eyes?

Time would pass for those two were it spent but in kissing each other; and time did pass.

But for Fuamnach—
She was brought to the Grianán of the Women, and to a private chamber; and she begged that Etain might be sent to her.

The magician was with her, and while they were yet alone she spoke to him eagerly, imperiously, supplicatingly.

" This is death for us both," the druid hissed.

Apart, in a corner of the room, he drew a little circle on the floor by the wall, and he stepped firmly into the circle.

" I shall not move from this spot," he said.

" There is no death," said Fuamnach. " It is well known. There is only removal."

" There is forgetfulness," said the druid bleakly. " There is wisdom to be learned all over again in the lower world, where all is hard to do, and where to be wise is harder than all else."

" You have your plan," said the harsh Queen. " Follow your plan and escape."

" I followed you . . .! " said Bresil.

And he turned upon her his bush of eye-brow and the scored pale mask of his face. And he stared upon her in surprise, as one stares and wonders at the prize for which death has been risked, and which is seen to be valueless.

" Do you desert me? " she whispered.

" No," said the grim man. " I stand by

161   M

you till success is sure, and, on that, I fly.
On that same instant I fly."

"You are good," she murmured. "You
are brave and good and loyal. I could adore
you for your goodness."

"Listen!" he admonished her. "We do
not seek to kill. We cannot kill, for life is
protected. She must be little enough to be
scarcely seen, and so light that she can be
blown beyond all bounds. For were she
left in this bound the Master of Magic could
find out where she was. . . .

"But there," said the magician, "there,
where she goes, he may not guess at her."

"Beyond air and water and fire," Fuamnach crooned in ecstasy. "Away beyond
it all. Out and out——"

"Hush!" said the druid.

And, on his word, Etain came in.

CHAPTER XII

THREE maids came with her, and their
presence was not welcome to the visitors.

But Fuamnach ran to meet her, and, with

a countenance that was all animation and joy, she kissed Etain.

"You have not changed," she said.

And, as she said it, a cold sword slipped into her heart; for indeed if Etain had changed it was for the better.

She had been lovely: she was yet more lovely; for she had supped on happiness and was cradled in delight. Now she trod like a queen. Youth and its grace were in her bearing. Beauty and its security were in her heart. Could she not be careless? In the two worlds what was there that she need consider?

She could return Fuamnach's kisses with the free laughter that she would bestow on the caresses of an infant or an animal; and she did so return them, breaking to a babble and ripple that was one half inquiries about her old home and one half the laughter of content and surprise. To not one answer that Fuamnach gave would Etain listen, but flung again another question and an hundred others.

"And you?" she inquired, her bright eyes dancing on Fuamnach.

"Ah, no!" Fuamnach laughed, as archly, "secrets can only be told in secret."

And her eyes also danced, but they danced
in the direction of the staring and whispering
maids, who were looking at her as with hawks'
eyes, and who would discuss her at leisure
as with adders' tongues.

They were waved from the room by Etain.

" Indeed," she said, " we should be
alone."

She did not yet notice Bresil Etarlaim, for
that man was effaced by his own bleak back-
wardness, and by the stir and chatter of
Fuamnach; so that, when these two sat,
Etain's back was to the druid, and she was
still, not unaware, but forgetful or rustled
into forgetfulness of his presence; for
Fuamnach did not leave one second without
its word, nor one half of a second without its
touch and bustle and caress.

CHAPTER XIII

Now had she seen the druid she would have
remarked him.

Nay, she would have uttered no word.
She would have fled, or her screams would

have brought the guard to her chamber as
though piled to it by an avalanche.

For the magician was looking at her with
his eyes shut.

His death's mask was staring at her. His
lean body was intended on her, and his blind
brow was freezing towards her.

He was away from her, and he was nearer
than her nerves. He was as intimately
within her as her own heart was. As a
worm slides to its hole, so he was sliding to
her mind. He was becoming her thought.

And she did think him, as one might
think a spear of ice; and she did feel him
as one might feel a tide of wintry water
splashed suddenly in the heart.

She went chill at an instant.

From her crown to her toes she withered
and wintered. She was bared of colour and
movement as a tree is bared of its leaves at
the hiss of a freezing blast.

Still she could see, she could still hear,
and it was Fuamnach that she saw and heard.

The lips that had suddenly tightened to a
string were murmuring " *Do not move,*" and
those eyes that became blazing suns and
sparkling pinpoints, that widened away in

black caves, and came back in white empti-
nesses, held her.

She could think of nothing but them.   She
could not think of them.   She could not
think of anything.

She was reduced of all that she had been.
She was an eye that looked, an ear that
listened.   She was an apprehension that
waited and expected.   She was a moaning
eagerness to do all that might be commanded, or to be all that should be permitted.

" Ah! " Fuamnach whispered to the ghost
of listening that remained.

" Ah, thief . . .!

" Do what you tell yourself to do.   Obey
your desire.   Fall, and fall and fall.   Be
winged.   Be but a wing.   Be lighter than
the wind.   Be but a living dust."

Agony ran in Etain's veins, and ecstasy
ran with it in her mind.   She willed to be
that which she was commanded.   She became a will; and, to the gigantic power
working without and within her, she added
all the strain and eagerness that was her own.

She would be free.   She would have wings.
She would drop grossness.   She would be
lighter than the very rumour of the wind.

Her pale lips wrenched and gaped. Her eyes fixed. Her hands clenched and shook, and her brow of pearl gathered and knotted and froze.

She sat in living stone . . .

She saw Fuamnach no more. She dreamed no more on surging and lapsing eyes, nor on a writhing red worm of a mouth.

She was utterly and monstrously alone. She was beyond sound and sight. She was beyond recall. She was beyond knowledge and all that touched on life.

She was in space with herself alone. . . .

She was a universe that thrilled in lightnings. That moaned in lightnings. . . . Green lightnings and red. Green soundless thunders. And a soundless roaring of red. . . .

Infinite space was about her: swooning and infinite; infinite and giddy and swooning. . . .

Before the eyes of Fuamnach her body blinked suddenly. It blew out like a blown-out flame. It disappeared.

" Behind me! " said the druid.

Fuamnach fled and crouched at his back;

167

her face rammed into her hands; her body shrinking into her shrinking shoulders.

" The wind! " she gasped.

And a wind came from that man's mouth.

A thin piercingness, that could be imagined but not felt. A thin chill, that could be shuddered at but not known. It swirled in the chamber like the rasp of a wasp's wing thrice repeated; and it was surmised no more but by the inward, remembering ear.

" It is done," said Bresil Etarlaim.

His teeth and his very bones were chattering, and he was but the grey shadow of a man as he stole to his feet.

" Out and out and out," Fuamnach stammered. " Out and away. Beyond air and water and fire. . . ."

She stood, she stared, she shuddered to the floor, and swooned there; while the grey druid crouched like a fox away.

CHAPTER XIV

To that room Angus and Midir came.

But the Master of Magic stood as though smitten, and paced a hasty step from that threshold.

" Do not go in," he cried. " There is death in the room."

And, to the servants who clustered around :

" Is the Queen, Etain, within? "

" She went within, Lord."

" If she has stayed within——! "

" She has not come out, Lord."

" She is lost! " he cried.

And, to the guards who would rush forward, " Do not dare that room."

He swung passionately on Midir.

" She is gone!   Etain is lost! "

" How! " cried the appalled King.

" Do not dare to enter," said Angus, " destruction is within."

But Midir grew lofty and proud.

" Have you forgotten my teachings? " he said.

" I had forgotten that you were the teacher," said Angus.

169

"Do not follow," he commanded the attendants. "Do not follow on your lives."

Then he and Midir stepped to the room and entered.

"There is nothing," Angus whispered.

"There is — something," said Midir. ". . . On the floor," he said.

And they strode to the corner of the room.

"Within a circle!" said Angus.

"Fuamnach!" cried Midir.

An instant they regarded the prone form. And, then, Fuamnach raised her body desperately on her hands. She stared into the eyes of Angus.

"Lord——!" she said.

"Where is Etain?" cried Midir. "Where is Etain?"

But she did not answer him. She did not look at him. She looked into the eyes of Angus.

"Lord——!" she whispered.

"Druidess!" said Angus. "She wolf—!"

His arm swept at her. Her head leaped bloodily from her shoulders, and thumped dully on the floor, and rolled.

Midir clapped his hands to his eyes.

" Oh! " he screamed.

" To the door," said Angus. " Quick, to the door! "

And, throwing aside the sword, with a frenzied hand he spun Midir from the room.

CHAPTER XV

So it was and such was the end of Fuamnach.

But for Etain the end was not yet; and when it would come, it would not be an end but a beginning. For it is so with all that seems forward; and if the eye could follow it would be seen that all things begin at the endings of all things, and that all that moves is an illusion.

The might of the druid, the will of Fuamnach, and her own will married to these, had done their work. Bulk and weight and space were taken from Etain. She could not be killed, and life must have a form to contain it, so she had been transformed to an insect; and when that wind came, and swirled the chamber, and swept away through the

171

open window, she had swirled with it, and with it had been swept away.

It was a wind that did not belong to the world of the Shí, and it could not stay there. It swept through that universe and out of and away from that universe. It left that world entirely and it brought the gathered insect with it. And, with the rasp of an angry wasp, it blew into this world of men, and the insect blew here with it.

When that wind was passing, the people of the house of Etar, lord of Inver Cichmaine in the north, were feasting on the flat roof of their fortress. They were drinking wine, and Etar's wife was sipping from a goblet. As the cup touched her lips the insect was dashed into it by the wind; and, before she could stop herself, she had drunk the wine and the insect.

" I have swallowed a fly," said she, and she stared with round eyes on her husband.

" All food fattens," said her merry consort.

But what was said in jest was true in fact; for the insect entered into her womb and abode there; and within the year Etain was reborn as the daughter of this lady.

But she was twelve hundred years of age

172

on the day that she was blown out of Faery, for, like other children, she was much older than she looked.

All children are lovely, but very few are beautiful. This child was lovely, and, so, winning. And she was beautiful, and, so, commanding. The fame of her loveliness would spread within miles of her home, for loveliness is localised and is only happy in circumscriptions. But as she grew, and as her beauty became apparent, that would become famous everywhere. For loveliness can be found in every village, but beauty is rarer than aught else, and the whole world is a-tiptoe for it.

" There is a distinction here," said Ailill.

" I also do not quite comprehend it," said Fergus.

" It is yet simple," Maeve replied. "Loveliness is a gentleness of the body and of the emotions, but beauty is a nobility of the mind."

A certain satisfaction and constraint came to the faces of the gentlemen present.

"I think," said Ailill, "that this distinction is very closely thought."

"It is possible," Maeve continued, "that beautiful men are not so rare as beautiful women."

"It may be as you say," said Fergus, looking very gently on the Queen, "yet I have seen a woman who is lovely and beautiful."

On him the Queen's eyes beamed, gentle as starlight.

"You are our treasure!" she said.

CHAPTER XVI

AT that time, and in this world, Eochaid Airem, the ninety-third monarch of Ireland, was ruling at Tara.

He was a young man, a young king, and the satisfactions that he required were so easily commanded that he did not for a long time think of marrying. When he was reminded, and that was frequent, that he could do so, he put the importunate matter away from him and forgot it.

174

But the subject has means even to restrain the King. The High King began to notice that his Court was not so populous with gentlemen as it had once been; and he was brought to observe this by discovering that ladies at his court were even scarcer than men.

No ladies were left to him, except those who were very old or very ugly or very tiresome.

He invented a feast, and commanded the nobility within reach of his messengers to attend him.

But his messengers brought back the intelligence that every gentleman of Ireland was ill, and that all their wives and daughters and nieces and sisters were ill also.

This was a disaster which a king would note.

Eochaid called a meeting of his Council, and when they met he saw that only those attended who were unmarried, or were widowers, or whose wives were of an excessive ugliness or of an unbelievable stupidity.

He was astonished and horrified when he saw the consorts that these statesmen brought with them. He uttered fiercely and regally his opinion of a world in which such females could occur; and expressed a preference for the torments of doom and death rather than that he should sit at the same banquet, or remain in the same building, or be discovered under the same sun with these ladies.

He forgot the matter for which his Council was called and rated his Assembly on their abominable marriages.

" What! " he said.

" Was the good earth not suited to your needs? Were the daughters of men so ill to ye that ye must rake in dens of the under-world for the hags and harridans and female-seeming abominations that ye have married?

" . . . Am I a king of ghouls? " he thundered. " Do I reign over miscreations and calamities?

" Ha! " he said.

" Were ye not mad to do it! Are ye not now mad to endure what ye have conjured!

" Unhappy wretches! Ye have blotted my reign. Ye have made me detest women! "

176

CHAPTER XVII

THE Councillors were reduced to tears by the wrath of the King, and by his terrible revelation touching their wives.

For each of these gentlemen had conceived that his wife could not possibly be as ugly as he imagined her to be. And each had further considered that the desolation which his wife caused to his soul was really traceable to the ill-condition of his own liver, or the too abundant noxiousness of his own bile.

" Majesty," one stammered, " it is not our fault."

" How, man? How may this be so? "

" Our mothers married us when we were young," said the weeping man.

" Idiot! " said the terse monarch. " Poltroon! " said he.

But a Councillor of them recovered his tongue :

" Majesty, no man can be excused for not marrying, for it is an evil abstention, and would be a treason to the State and to life itself."

" So! " said Eochaid.

" And no man can be blamed for marrying," another urged, " for he is too young to know what he is doing, and too gay to care about it."

" I am young," said the King. " I am gay. Do I marry obnoxiously? Do I go wooing with my eyes closed and my heart asleep? No mother has married me," he thundered.

" Your Mightiness," said one, who had been cut to the quick by the King's opinion of his wife, " your Mightiness must shortly go the way of all men, and be married as his mother or the gods dictate."

" What! "

" It is so. And when the wife of your Magnificence grows as old as ours are, she will be as little desirable as ours are; and the King will care as little about it as I do."

And this man glared truculently and detestingly on his humbled fellows.

But Eochaid stood to his supreme height, and he blazed carelessly upon that man as the sun blazes on a yelping dog.

" Do you insult the King? " said he. " Or is it only that you threaten him? "

" Neither, Majesty. I only advise the King."

" Ah ! " said Eochaid, and he rang forth a huge laughter.

" Do you advise the High King? "

" By law," that man stammered. " By the law of All Ireland, I am a King's Adviser."

" By law ! " said Eochaid, and he sat again; but his levelled and challenging brows were not good to see.

" Advise us now," he said, " and let us hear what it will sound like. By my hand ! " quoth he, " we have never been advised before."

The abashed Councillor drew a deep and distant breath.

" Majesty," he said, " I advise that your Majesty get married."

But Eochaid laughed uproariously.

" Ah no ! no ! no ! You cannot get me into your clann by that path. Do not try, Councillor, to be any man's mother; and try, least of all, to be the King's."

" Yet," said the noble hurriedly, " it is yet the advice of all your Councillors."

" And has been these five years back," said an emboldened comrade.

" I remember," said the King genially.

179

" It has been suggested before. We will
not speak of it any more."

The Council stirred uneasily, but no man
of them dared to continue.

CHAPTER XVIII

" LORDS," said Eochaid, " your advice is
sought and will be welcomed on another
matter. A plague has fallen upon our
realm. Our messengers report that the
whole land, men and women, are dying. We
wish to learn more of this, and to know what
ye have done against this pestilence."

The smile that trembled on one aged lip
was communicated to others as venerable;
and the King was amazed to see that nothing
but his own royal presence restrained these
Councillors from uproarious laughter.

He stared, and, as far as a King might be
so, he was bewildered. But he was as direct
in speech as in action.

"Have I made a joke?" he asked hopefully.

" Your Majesty is always witty," a lord
answered.

" Have I been wittier than usual? " said the King.

" It would scarcely be possible," said that Councillor. " But," he continued, " the matter of this pestilence has come to us curiously after the question of your royal marriage."

" Ah yes," said the King, " yes, it is very funny."

" For your royal marriage——"

" We will leave that where it is," said Eochaid, " and discuss this less comical business."

" They are so intimately connected, Sir, that they cannot be considered apart from each other."

" Ah! " said Eochaid.

And he propped his head upon his hands, and stared with wide eyes and a pursed mouth upon the speaker.

" There is actually no sickness in the land," the Councillor continued.

" There is no sickness! " said Eochaid.

" The nobles of Ireland have come to the conclusion that until your Majesty is married they cannot afford to be your Majesty's guests."

A pale wind of wrath seemed to touch Eochaid's cheek, and, as his lip lifted, a white tooth shone fiercely from it at that gathering.

" So! " he said.

" It is so, Majesty.   Until your Majesty is married no gentleman of Ireland will come to your Court.   No gentleman of Ireland will permit his wife, his daughter or his sister to come to Tara until the King is married."

But Eochaid's eyes were a bushed-in stare of rage, and his mouth was a thin-drawn menace.

" It is treason," he snarled.

" It is not treason, Lord.   The Throne is safe, and the King's person is unapproachable; but the King is exacting more than his most loving subject can tolerate; and this Council, in its duty, advises the Throne to be as loving of its subjects as its loving subjects deserve."

" The Council is ended," said Eochaid.

CHAPTER XIX

AFTER three months of an extraordinary abstinence the King capitulated. By virtue of many raging discussions with others, and of much private reasoning with himself, he came more to consider the advice of his Councillors and the wishes of his people.

Except for very young men, he could find nobody who was of his opinion on the subject that racked his heart. But it was from a conversation with his mother that his conversion commenced.

" This has never happened to a King before," he said, as he sprawled gloomily in the Royal Grianán.

" Son," she said, " it has happened to every King before."

" Do you think so? " he asked, staring.

" I truly do, and more, it will happen to every King that will follow you."

" No? " said Eochaid.

" It certainly will," said his mother, " for it is in the nature of things."

Eochaid stared down the long succession of monarchs that should succeed him.

183

"The poor boys!" he said.   "The poor, poor boys!"

His mother looked severely from her embroidery.

"If you do not get married, my Lamb, there will be no poor boys to lament over."

"By my hand!" said Eochaid.

He examined her and that statement as in a trance.

"It is perfectly true," he cried.   "I shall immediately get married," said he.

He leaped to his feet, and it seemed to the royal lady that he was about to summon the guard and demand that a wife be hauled to him.

"Do nothing precipitate, my child," she begged him.   "Leave this delicate matter to me.   I know——"

"No, mother," he said firmly.   "I know all the girls that you like, and I do not like them.   They all snivel when they speak: they all giggle when they look——"

"Oh, son!" said the queen-mother. "Oh, child!"

"It is true," he said.   "It is exactly so."

"It is not so," she answered firmly.

184

" I have seen them all, mother. I would sooner be bedded with a bramble bush than with any one of them."

" Child! " she said.

" I would rather marry the queen of the bees and die of it than touch, even with a stick, one friend of your friends."

" The Throne must be considered," she insisted. " The King cannot marry out of his rank. Your mother is the only person who can choose your wife."

" Oh! " cried Eochaid, and he leaped to his feet.

A vision came to him of the wives that his Councillors' mothers had married to his Councillors, and his soul blenched at the sight, and at the thought that he might be mothered into a matrimony like theirs.

" Ha! " he said, " if one must be married by his mother or by the gods, I shall be married by the gods. It is more dignified," he said.

Within the hour his runners were out, and a chase began among them that took in all Ireland; and a competition was aroused between them the earnestness of which, and

the deadliness of which, had never before
been known in the land.

They were looking for the most beautiful
woman in Ireland.

Nor was it only the treasure which the
winner would receive that spurred them, nor
the fiery command of the King.

Their mettle as men was aroused; and
each of them murmured to his heart—" I
know a beautiful woman when I see one, and
I shall know the most beautiful woman when
I see her."

" Such an one," the runner conceived,
tugging on his chariot line, and drenching
his soul in bliss—" Such an one will be of
such an age; of such a complexion; of such a
slendering curve; of such——"

The chariots dashed wildly among dreams,
and all of the charioteers were in love.

CHAPTER XX

" THIS is an excellent story," said Fergus
mac Roy, " and I am full of curiosity as to
what follows."

" It is curious indeed," Maeve replied.

" I perceive also," said Fergus, " that this King was not born to be happy."

" He was not happy," said Maeve thoughtfully, " but, also," she said, " he was not unhappy."

" It should be so," said Fergus. " We must hear how he further bore himself."

" Thus," said Maeve.

Although Etain lived in the small household of a chief, she was yet trained in greatness. Her father and mother idolised her, for with them she was lovely and loving and gentle. And all their people, and the people of all that neighbourhood, adored her. Their hearts were warmed by her as by a cordial, for she was beautiful and noble, with a distant speech, and a regard that was distant and kindly. She could remember them beautifully, and as beautifully, and in their presence, she could forget them. Beauty was so about her that none could harm her nor be hurt by her. She was loved thoughtlessly, hopelessly, beautifully, as the sun or a flower is loved; and if she read ever in a young man's eye she read love there and no other thing.

Now Etain had a certain habit, and I, myself, have the same habit, for it is hereditary in our family, and falls within our geasa. The habit was that she would only bathe or cleanse herself in running water; by, that is, a river, a well or a spring.

Early on a day she betook herself to a well that lay outside her father's fortress. She was unattended, for she was in the habit of going to this well ever since she was a child.

She set out carrying in one hand her golden comb, and a napkin; and in the other hand her silver basin that had four golden birds perched on its edges and was set cunningly with small blue stones—And that basin, said Maeve complacently, is now my own basin, in which I wash every day.

She had washed herself, and braided again her hair, and only delayed going home because the sun was shining, and because it was pleasant to lie in the grass listening to the splash and chuckle of the water, and dreaming distantly and unintelligibly, as all girls do.

Dreaming so, she heard the clatter of chariot wheels, and there came along the road and towards where she sat, a royal chariot, the

like of which this countryside had never seen;
and it was drawn by four horses so slender
and proud and active that Etain of the Steeds
could not but regard them with delight.

The chariot halted, and the charioteer,
bearing the golden fillet of his office round
his brow, came towards the well. But in a
moment the lord of that chariot dismounted
also, and he too came striding to the well.

He was mightily noble and beautiful. He
trod like a king, and he stared royally on the
girl, whose heart set to so unexpected a beating that it flooded her cheeks and lips with
rosy fire.

CHAPTER XXI

IT is not fitting that runners or the base-born
should meddle in great affairs, and it was not
the runners who found a wife for Eochaid.

While they were abroad, and during the
month of their seeking, Eochaid went to visit
his territories in the north. The journey had
been long and his horses were hot. When
the King noticed that they were uneasy he
called to the driver:

189

" Give the animals to drink," he said.

And the driver drove aside to find a well.

Soon they came to one. The Charioteer
dismounted to water the horses, and Eochaid
descended also, for there was a girl before
him at the well.

Beside her was a silver basin that had four
golden birds perched upon it, and there were
bright purple stones set in the rim of the
basin. A purple cloak with long silver
fringes was lying by her on the grass. Her
dress was of green silk, and falling along it
behind was a long hood embroidered in gold.
On each breast, just deep enough to hold
them, there was a little cup of gold; and on
each of her shoulders was a narrow silver clasp.

The sun was shining upon her, and indeed,
with her dress and her basin and her choice
ornaments she was shining back again at
the sun.

But it was not only her gear that shone.
Brighter than the flashing of gold and silver
was the shining of her yellow hair. She
wore it in two great golden plaits, and there
were four locks in each plait, and at the end
of each lock a precious bead was twinkling.

Eochaid saw all this, for he was looking

with all his eyes, and he was filled with consternation.

Her snowy arms were out through the sleeve holes of her vest, and her hands, long and delicate and agile, were raised to the great tresses. Her hands and arms were white as snow, and her brow as white again; and beneath this were two eyes of a deeper, a softer blue than Eochaid had ever imagined that he could see; and beneath again, two lips, half opened in surprise, and red as the rowan berry, were looked at long by Eochaid.

The soft light of the moon was in her face: the light of pride was on her brow; and to each cheek there came, and went, and came again, a dimple of delight, as she observed the mighty young man who had become all eyes and no tongue; and who stood and stared and could find no word to say, or could find only words that were an utter incomprehensibility.

Indeed the young King blushed and trembled and stammered and no longer knew what he should or should not do.

But Etain blushed and did not tremble, though she looked on a youth and a magnificence that were the equal of her own.

At a stroke Eochaid ceased to be all that he had been.

He was a man no more, he was a lover. He was a King no more, he was a lover.

That is, he was a person filled with astonishment and alarm and delight.

He was astonished to consider how very wonderful a girl could be. He was alarmed to discover how unworthy he was even to look at this girl. He was delighted to conceive that this girl and this girl alone should be his bride.

He demanded her name and revealed his own. He demanded her abode, and would go there with her; and the people of that neighbourhood were alarmed to see their treasure whirling past them in a chariot so beautiful, and drawn by steeds so marvellous, and inhabited by beings so glorious, that they could have imagined that the horses and the chariot and the occupants could only be matched in Faery, and must have come thence.

Eochaid saw the parents of his beloved; and, when he set out on the next day, Etain and her people and a cavalcade went with him.

192

For how could there be delay when the High King frowned and thundered and was astonished that delay could be in any matter that was personal to himself?

They were bound for Tara of the Kings, The Lofty City, The Secret Place of the Road of Life.

CHAPTER XXII

EOCHAID said all the things to Etain that should be said, for he was one who would utter all that was in his heart; and she listened to his explanations and admonishments with a gay wonder.

Looking on him, she discovered that she did not dislike hearing of these things. She came more and more to be surprised at the interest such explanations could hold, and was even more astonished at the difficulty she had in exhausting her own curiosity concerning them.

For she felt that, at whatever cost to the mind, she must comprehend exactly what it was that Eochaid meant.

His words she gathered abundantly.   But, while he spoke them, and when he looked at her, there was that in his eye, there was that in his fingers, that did not stumble into his speech.

" You are the Bright Branch of Fortune," said Eochaid.   " You are the White Sapling of the Bright-Stemmed Wood.   I love you," said Eochaid.

" You do? " she insisted.

" By my soul, by my hand," said Eochaid.

" But how do you love me? " said Etain, and she listened intently, craftily, suspiciously.

The young King drew a vast breath into his lungs, and then he puffed it monstrously and helplessly abroad.

" Thus! " he said; and he smote mightily on his bosom.

" In that way! " said Etain.

And her eyes beamed into his so sweetly, so trustingly, that he scarce dared to look at them, and would have died rather than look away.

He would take her hand in his and gaze upon it in a very stupor of attention; and with the same amazement he would examine her hair and her cheek.

" She is a Beloved Love! " he said.

And at times, when he closed his eyes, and sought with blind lips forward, it seemed to Eochaid that something was happening that had never before happened in the world.

And, when her lips were found, he thought that here was an inexhaustible fountain; and that here one might drink all thirst away, all remembrance away, all but life itself away; for this was life.

And at times, yearningly, supplicatingly, holding her hands in his, and her eyes with his own, he would say:

" My little Branch! my Dove! do you truly love Eochaid? "

And she, held thus, and never feeling the bond, would reply:

" Indeed and indeed, I love you dearly."

" You do not call me Your Branch," said broken-hearted Eochaid. " You do not call me Your Lamb."

" Indeed and indeed I do," said Etain. " You are my own Branch, you are my Lamb."

CHAPTER XXIII

THE bride-price was paid, the ceremonies were completed, and they were married; and whether the King or his people were the happier no man can say.

But, day by day, Eochaid awoke to a new delight.

Now the world was fair.

Now the sun did shine.

And what a moon was now that moon that beamed the night to beauty!

How lovely, how lonely was the world!

How wonderfully was it filled with all that did not trouble!

Clouds and men!   Birds and flowers and women!   They were, they vanished, and were again when they were sought.

Sleek little creatures, that were sinuous and shining, showed their shy curvetings to Eochaid in the wood.   Bushy and shaggy things were robust and affectionate to him in the plain.   In every tree a bird was singing for Eochaid; and every bush swung marvels for him in the air.   And the air itself spun

196

shimmerings and jewellings to the grass, to the sky, to the heart—Yea, and to all that was deeper and unknown.

And, with one closing of an eye, all these could vanish!

With one closing of a door all these were swept away, and there was—Etain!

Nay, Etain and Eochaid remained.

They were not alone: they were together. They were not lonely: they were together. They were not uncared for: they cared for one another. And because they cared for each other the earth must care for them, and the wide world love them because they loved each other. Separation might be for those who can be separated; and unhappiness for such as know not how to love. Life! what was it? Death! 'twas but a name. But for Etain and for Eochaid, there was no separation: there was no unhappiness: there was no more death or conjecture. There was love and loving and loveliness. There was their stir in a waiting world. Their eyes in a universe that thrilled to see them. Their lips, and the space where these could meet . . . And elsewhere, everywhere, there was Etain, there was Eochaid.

How could he tire explaining to her that he loved his kingdom, his people, his life; and that more than these again he loved Etain!   And how could she but doubt him; and seek to entrap him in an insufficient utterance; and lie in wait for a lazy look that she could blame, or an unlyrical utterance that could astound her.

Indeed he had but scant time to discover if deeply and truly she loved him, although he moaned to her to tell him that, and to seal the telling with another miracle of her regard, and a newer miracle of her lip or hand.

CHAPTER XXIV

THE feast that had been given to celebrate the wedding was ended, and when the guests went away the King's happiness was clouded.

For these people could no longer see his Etain.   She could only be seen by those, the guards, the servants, whose busynesses must prevent them from properly observing her.

Eochaid demanded, invented, another

feast, and was not contented until the
chariots came rolling in, and he could see
how the women were astonished and dis-
mayed at the sight of his queen; and how
the men were astonished and entranced,
and were forgetful of their wives, and were
even forgetful of the King, when once they
looked upon the noble, the long-limbed,
winsome lady.

He would awaken this comrade from a
gape of beatitude with a great push of the
shoulder, and a royal reproof.

" Ha! Are those the manners that are
current in the south? "

Or:

" What, friend, what! Are fair women
scarce in Connacht? "

Or, like a careful and skilful father, he
would admonish another:

" To stare at his own wife and to be loyal
to the King, these are two good deeds."

And these nobles would look at him
desolately, dumbfoundedly, and would go
apart to be alone, to be discontented and
peevish, and to dream of the emptiness of
life.

And at the ladies, whom aforetime he had

thought to be fabricated by magicians of the Shí, he looked appraisingly, almost disdainfully. And he saw that this lip of wonder was commendable, and yet but a palish thing; and that the shoulder yonder that could uphold a world was prize enough for the lordling who mourned by it, but was not equal to the terrible majesty of the crown.

Among the guests there came Eochaid's younger brother Ailill, known afterwards as Aenguba, of the One Fault. He, too, looked on the Queen, and he was admitted to, but did not greatly avail himself of, the intimacy that should be given to a brother.

When the guests had departed Eochaid observed the boy's ill looks.

" Ailill," he said, " you are not well? "

And he was astounded as he said it, for the men of his family were such as illness dared never attack.

" Indeed, brother," said Ailill, " I do not think that I am very well."

" You are pale and wasted; the pith is gone out of your bones, and you are only half of the half of a man. What does this mean? "

" It is an illness," Ailill replied.

"An illness! Ha! by my hand!" cried Eochaid.

And he would have forbidden that illness, but that the appearance of his brother distressed him. He addressed himself threateningly to illness, and put a protecting arm about the boy's shoulders.

"You shall stay with me," he said comfortingly. "Etain will nurse you. There shall be no more of these illnesses," he said; and he uttered an "Ha!" terribly upon the air.

He went to his wife's Grianán.

"My Love! My Bird! My One Lamb!" he said.

"No," Etain replied firmly. "You have said my Love, my Bird, my Lamb, a thousand times. There is no honour in words that are thus easily and habitually repeated."

"My Berry of the Mountain," Eochaid recommenced hopefully.

"It is said to every girl in the world," cried Etain, and it seemed indeed that she would and must weep. And at this Eochaid's soul became filled with utter desolation. He beat mightily upon his bosom, and thundered forth in despair, "I love thee, Etain! Etainín, I love but thee!"

" But how do you love me? " said Etain.

And thereon Eochaid drew a vast breath into his lungs, and puffed it hugely and helplessly abroad.

" Thus! " he said, and he smote mightily on his breast.

" You love me exactly so? " his wife demanded.

" In that way alone," cried Eochaid.

" But," he said, and a monstrous misery came upon him, " you do not call me Your Love! Your Lamb! Your One Bird! "

" Indeed and indeed I do," said Etain. " You are My Love! My Own, Own Lamb! You are My One Bird! "

CHAPTER XXV

" I had forgotten," said Eochaid.

" What have you forgotten," the Queen murmured, for in truth her forgetfulnesses coincided with his own, and they willed to and would forget everything but each other.

" My brother! "

" We will remember him again," Etain

coaxed. " In a little little time we can remember everything again."

" I am in trouble," said Eochaid.

" Do not be in trouble," she said. " You must not be troubled."

" He is ill," said Eochaid. " He is sick," said he.

And he and Etain meditated profoundly this strange news.

" I must go away in a few days to visit my princes," Eochaid continued, " and I am afraid that while I am gone the boy may die."

" Oh! " said the Queen.

" He looks like one about to die," said Eochaid. " I put my arm about his shoulder and he nigh sank under it: he is wasted and pale, and he only stands by his great spirit."

" Alas! "

" I told him that you would nurse him."

" I will surely do so," she answered.

" And that that would make him well."

" My Lamb! " said Etain. " I could make you well, no matter how ill you were."

" You could surely raise me from the dead."

" But how could I make another man

203

well?" she asked, and she spread her hands piteously abroad.

"Your hands!" said Eochaid, regarding them with delight. "Your eyes!" he cried, marvelling upon them. "I am sure that you can save him," he said pleadingly. "I am quite certain that you can cure him."

"I will do all that I can," she murmured.

"And if he dies——" said Eochaid, and went darkly silent.

"See that his games are played. See that his stone is raised, with the ogham deeply carved telling of his rank, and that we loved him.

"He shall not die," cried Etain fiercely. "I will not permit him to die."

"I told him so," Eochaid exploded. "I told him exactly so, but he did not look as if he believed me: he smiled and tottered away, and when I called to know where he was going, he answered that he was going to his bed."

"I will cure him," said Etain. "I will not let our brother die."

On this Eochaid took heart, and he set out to visit his territories, and to confer with his princes.

CHAPTER XXVI

As for Ailill:

He had indeed taken to his bed, and he wasted there daily, almost hourly. When Etain went to visit him she was horrified to see how woeful the boy looked.

His cheeks had fallen into two blue caves; his hair matted upon that thin paleness gave him the aspect of death itself; and beneath the bedclothes his body was but one long bone.

As she stood staring upon this ruin of youth, Etain fell to a surmise and a speculation that thrilled and terrified her. For, already, Ailill was not of the world; and she could imagine, in panic, that it was thus death came, and that it would, and in every despite, draw thus at last to her, and to all else that lived.

The men, she thought, and the beasts and the trees, they will all die! They are all dying now! and in every part and parcel of the earth all that is living is dying by slow inches, and will be gone in a little while, and be never again remembered.

And she saw herself thus touched one day,

and she shivered in terror of that touch. And she saw that others would stand about her bed as she stood now by Ailill's, with their hands hanging helplessly, and with their minds regarding her, helplessly. And she foresaw that she would slip from among them, on a long sigh, while yet they would not know if she had or had not gone.

To be so full of strength, and yet to be full merely of helplessnesses! Was it not a wrong, and a mockery of all that seemed real!

She looked on the carved and rigid face that lived now only in its eyes; and she saw them, immense and sombre; dark pits of dream and resignation. And she saw that they and the dream were looking at her searchingly, pleadingly.

Before that gaze she banished thought, and, so far as might be, she banished helplessness.

She bent above the boy, and she smiled her life at him and into him. She laughed it into his eyes; and into her laugh she would pack all that was hers of beauty and vivacity and command.

" Dear Ailill! " she said.

" You are better already," she said.

But he closed his eyes upon her.

She could see him no more; she could only see his mask; and he could not see her.

He was withdrawn; he had withdrawn himself, or was withdrawn by death.

Against those closed eyes, and over that closed face, her spirit beat vainly. She could not unlock them, nor uncarve one line of the doom that was graven there.

She went away trembling and terrified, and she said to her soul:

" Of what use am I? "

And she said to her soul:

" Of what use is anything? "

He was young, and he was dying! and yet the physicians told her that he had no disease.

"What is it?" she stormed, and she would impress violently on the Chief Physician the wisdom that he had not got.

" There is nothing wrong with the prince," said Fachtna. " He is merely dying."

" But one does not die thus," she cried, wringing in her hands an anguish that was intolerable.

"One does," Fachtna replied. "One dies because one wants to die."

"One does not want to die," said Etain.

"Or because we want something that we will not live without."

"What is there that a man can want in that fashion?"

"He will not tell me," the physician answered. "He will not tell his secret to anybody."

But Etain cut fiercely into his abstraction.

"He shall tell it to me," she cried, "and if the thing that he wants can be found in the world I will get it for him."

CHAPTER XXVII

"I AM an old man," said the physician. "I have seen much of life and death and all that lies between them; and, if it be only through my own sons, I can remember youth, and all that it craved for, and much of what it was willing to die for."

"You would have many memories," said Etain, meditating on that domed brow and on the peaceful eyes that made it lovely.

" There are two things that can bring youth to death."

" And those? "

" Vanity can cause a young man to die, and love can kill him."

" Love could kill me.   It is surely true," said the Queen.

" We know our Ailill," said the doctor, rising and pacing the room. " He has grown up amongst us, and there is no better boy in the world.   He is proud, but he is not vain. There is not one vice in his heart.

And, saying so, he sat again, bending his love where he could not bend his mind.

" You think that he is in love! " said Etain.

" He is beyond my aid."

" He is not beyond all aid," she said. " There is help for him somewhere.   Wherever the woman that he loves may be his life is there, and she can save him if she can be found."

" He will not breathe one word of her," said Fachtna.   " She is his rune, his deadly secret.   He closes his eyes and goes back-

209   P

wards within himself, to her, to his heart, to
his death."

" Ah! " said Etain.

And now she trod the room all a flame of
excitement and inspiration.

" You do not know how to ask.   You are
only a man, and what does a man know of
men . . .?   If it were a maid, how quickly
you could unlock her lips . . . but a man will
tell you nothing; he would be ashamed to
tell it to a man.

" It may be so."

" I shall be his doctor, and his confidant;
and you shall see how good a doctor Etain is."

" If you can make him speak," said the
doctor, " he will be already half cured by the
mere speaking; he will give away something
of his burden by only talking of it; and if he
tells it twice he will give it all away."

" He shall speak twice and thrice," said
Etain.   " He shall give it all away."

" Go, you," she continued, and she was
all urgency and resolve.   " Prepare him for
my visit.   Tell him that he must be nice to
me.   Tell him that I am the Queen, and
that he must be nice to the Queen.   Say
that his dear sister is coming, and that he

must be nice to her.   Tell him these things
even though he will not listen to you; and
send me word to come the instant you have
told them."

"Good!" said the doctor.   "I shall say all
these things, and it may be that his sister will
do him more good than I or my brethren
can do."

CHAPTER XXVIII

SHE went again to his bed, whereto she had
now gone so many times, and from which so
many times she had returned stricken with
fear and helplessness.   Now her hands were
not helpless, for there was something she
could attempt, and perhaps that she could do.

"Whoever he yearns for!" said Etain,
"I will surprise her name from him, and if
she has to be dragged here in chains, here
she shall come; and all that she can give shall
be given or I will murder her."

"Ha!" she thought, and the very thunder
and accent of Eochaid rang in her thought;
"am I the Queen or am I not!"

And she darted her mind abroad like a

fiery sword, threatening that unknown woman
and daring her to be disobedient.

" If Eochaid were here," she pondered,
" how he would rate that woman.   How he
would overbear her, and impress his will upon
her as a thumb is sunk into wax.   She
should run, she should fly, to do all that he
commanded; and she shall run, shall fly for
me, and shall do all that I order her to do."

" Ailill, My Pulse!" she said.   " My dear
Ailill! "

And her voice was low as a little wind, and
gentle and intimate as the song of a bird to
his near-by mate.

" Will you not open your eyes for me? Do
you no longer love Etain? "

His eyes did open, and she was looked at
by a dream; a dream that shivered upon her
and about her; and that was all of love and
death and farewell.

" My dear one! " she said, " do you not
love me? "

At the words his eyes awakened, as though
they had been blown into flame, and he
searched vainly in that candid face, as an
hunted man seeks vainly for a place to hide in.

"I am dying," he said. "Oh! I am dying!"

"Love does not kill," she crooned. "Love does not die."

"How did you know?" he whispered.

"Am I not a woman?" said Etain.

And now a trembling and a great shaking took hold of Ailill, as though death had clutched him by the throat and would shake his life out.

"You do not love me!" he gasped. "You cannot possibly love me!"

A bell of horror rang one dizzying peal in Etain's ears. Her lips opened, but ere that scream could come she dashed her face to the bed and strangled it, and she remained there, one quake of unconsciousness, and of unutterable listening.

She could hear that thin, whispering ecstasy:

"Etain! Etain! Oh, Etain!"

She could feel his fingers moving to her head, moving into her hair: and again she heard his voice:

"Etain! Etain!"

She lifted her head, and her pale lips smiled

213

at him, and her eyes, heavy with dream and resignation, beamed kindly upon him.

But, ere she could speak, she must swallow, again and again, as though it was a mountain that she must swallow.

" Ailill, my beloved! " she said. " My poor Ailill! "

" The High King! " he stammered.

" I will give you all that you desire," she said.

" My brother! " he said; and Etain closed her eyes.

" I will give you all that you desire," she said.

A great shuddering came upon them both, and for a long time they remained with closed eyes, and there was nothing vital within them but that trembling.

CHAPTER XXIX

So Ailill began to get well.

The physicians wondered at it. Everybody wondered at his swift retreat from the very gripe of death; and they thought that there must be magic in Etain's hands, or in her eyes or voice.

It was known that the hands of a king could heal even desperate diseases, but the hands of a queen were not credited with the same virtue. So people wondered, and came to her with their illnesses, and, because they believed that she could cure them, they cured themselves, and, so, were cured by her.

Day after day she sat by Ailill's bed, and the beam of love that she had shown to him was always in her eyes, and the hand that had been gentle in his was never withdrawn from his hand that sought it.

But she did not speak much.

It seemed to her that words were difficult or unnecessary things: nor could she remember many of them; and those that she could remember did not seem appropriate.

For, at times, as from a void, words would arise, unbidden, unsought:

" My Love! my Bird! my Lamb! " her heart would say, or they would be uttered in her heart.

But these she could not repeat.

These were words that belonged elsewhere; that were sacred to one who was

215

absent. Nay, they would not be understood by any other than that absent one.

And when, in that dream-laden stillness, she felt that her hand was pressed by a fevered hand, and heard a whisper, again and again and again, "Etain! Oh, Etain! I love you, Etain!" words again floated about her as at vast distances, dim wraiths of speech:

"How do you love me? Tell me exactly how you love me?"

But she could not say those words, for they could only be said to one who was absent, and could only be sensible to him.

Her kind eyes must do all her talking.

"Dear Ailill!" she would say.

And again:

"I knew you would get well."

"For you," he said. "It is only for you."

"I knew that I could cure you," she said.

And she roused her soul, so that her eyes laughed and her lips laughed, and her hands laughed within his; and he was all a tease and an exasperation, and a will to be better quicker than even a miracle could do it.

But his recovery was rapid as his illness had been.

A day came when the tall youth was no

longer in bed. And another when he strode in the corridors, and would venture to the fields. And the day arrived when all that had been promised should be paid.

" To-night! " said Ailill.

His eyes were shining, and his voice was a dry huskiness, and he scarce dared hear his own whisper.

" To-night I shall be in the palace garden: in the druid's hut: he will be absent. . . . To-night . . .! "

" He will be absent," Etain thought. " He is with the King! "

She raised her head, and she stared royally on the boy. An eye that he had never seen before regarded him, and it was as though he were looked on by an eagle.

In her mind the very thunder and accent of an absent one was rolling.

" By my hand! " said her proud soul.

But her lips said nothing. They smiled suddenly, gently, reassuringly, and her mind that had pondered him thought:

" He will die again if that is withheld that was promised."

217

CHAPTER XXX

THE night came with no moon and with never a star.

A night of dark silence and dark whisperings; and through it Etain made her way.

Now, for the first time, her heart knew panic, heard panic, was panic.

Now it was not only her eyes that strove vainly to pierce abroad. Her being was the fortress of an hundred sentinels, all desperately peering, and clamouring all that they could not see, and that they could be seen.

With what strung diligence she listened!

Had she really thought that she was a mass of blind eyes, she who was all ears, that were clogged and unclogged in infinite speeds and successions! So that at times she heard nothing, and the world was dead; and ere that thought was come the thunder of silence that had deafened her was superseded, and she heard more than could be audible, or than mortal ear might gather.

A branch creaked and screamed at her!

A terrified bird and her terrified heart flew on the one spurt of fear!

218

She said:

" There is nothing here but darkness: I cannot be seen.   There is nothing here but silence. There is not a soul at this hour abroad."

But every shadow held within it a deeper, a menacing shade.   And, within it, every silence hid a silence that could roar.

She came to the druid's hut, and stood, staring on the oaken door that she could feel but could scarcely see, and that would open at but a pressure.   Draped all in the darkness of her mantle and of the night she stood gazing so, with her hand upraised one inch from the door.

She peered to each side and behind her, and in each way she saw an infinite blackness; and she looked above to a troubled nothing that was black and grey; that was no colour; that was not dark enough to be invisible, nor light enough to be known.

She intended her fingers against the door, but did not touch it; for her heart spoke to her, suddenly, neatly, cleanly, in the darkness:

" My Love! my Bird! my Lamb! " her heart said.

And she was astonished.

She smiled chidingly at her heart, as one smiles at a pet animal that has committed a little fault; and she pressed on the door.

So slowly she pressed, and it so slowly opened. She pressed on it with such a gentle, persistent earnestness that it could not but open, slowly, slowly, as her slim hand willed it.

She saw a light. A thin rod of the palest gold was looked at by her: a bar of ruddier gold was deeply examined; and, with another push, there was a broad shining that flickered, and swayed, and retreated, and crept again.

She looked at the one torch that burned in an angle of the wall, and she closed the door.

She looked to the other side, where an oaken chair stood by an oaken table; and behind, where, in an alcove, there was a pallet of fern and straw, with a leathern coverlet thrown over it, and a fleece crumpled on it by the wall.

Except herself there was no person in the room.

She did not remove the dark hood in

which her face, milk-white against the stuff, was framed.

Her eyes ran everywhere, and soon her noiseless feet were flitting, flitting—from the door to the table, from the table to the torch, from the torch to the pallet.

She sat on the pallet, and, in an agony of impatience, she wrung her breasts in hands that were as tender.

She did not say, " He does not come! "

She said:

" It is not done! It is not done! "

She ran to the torch, and beat it on the floor; and, from it, she ran again to the pallet. She crouched there, shutting her eyes against a very desolation of darkness that filled that room.

She listened for a cautious footfall, for the tiny creaking of a pressed-on door.

She heard the very desolation of silence.

She heard her own listening.

She heard the mournful utterance of her heart, ticking surprise as a clock ticks time—

" It is not done! It is not done! "

CHAPTER XXXI

On the next day she saw Ailill.

She was not angry. She was filled with astonishment, and when his hand stretched for hers she let it be taken, and did not utter a word.

She looked at him with her lips pursed to a red bud of inquiry, and her eyes wide with marvelling, and she saw that the young man was drowned in despair, and that he could scarcely speak. Suddenly she was filled with terror for him.

" Dear Ailill! " she said.

He wrung his hands, and it was as though he wrung his soul.

" I could not come," he said. " My servant, my foster-brother, prepared everything, and I waited here for the hour to come. It came, and on that instant I fainted, and I have lain in a faint through all that dreadful night."

" Dear Ailill——! " she said.

Her lips were dry and her breath was oppressing her.

" To-night! " he said.

" Oh! " she gasped.

" It was just a chance," said Ailill. " It can never happen again. Look, I am full of health and vigour. It was my own thought, my own great love that undone me. I will not think of it nor of you for all this day."

He smiled swiftly at her and was as instantly grave and urgent.

" To-night! " he said, and he kissed her hands, and clung desperately to them.

Again she went to the hut.

But now she was not affrighted by darkness or by silence. She did not see the one nor hear the other. She did not lack the moon, nor heed that she might or might not be followed.

She was a turmoil and a flooding of impatience.

There was that to be done, that had been promised. There was that to be given, that had been promised; and she must do and give.

But she was willing, she was eager to do it all, to give it all.

" Ailill . . .! " she thought.

And her mind fled from him and to him like two fleetings of lightning.

So quickly had it moved! And yet there had been time for her spirit to bathe itself in a distant tenderness; and in the flying return of her mind, she bestowed that tenderness on him she was to meet.

" Dear Ailill——! " she said.

And her feet broke to a run.

She must not be late. He might die if she were even one minute late.

He loved her! How he did love her! If he but knew how anxious she was! If he but knew that she was . . . running to him!

She reached the hut. She swung open the door.

She ran in.

He was not there.

The torch was burning, and she saw again the oaken table, and the pallet by the wall.

" I am too early," she said. " I am all out of breath with running," she said to herself. " I will wait for him."

She tossed her hood aside; and the room was lit by her; by her silken and silvern shimmerings; by the flashing gold of her hair, and by the snowy whiteness of her arms.

She did not even close the door.

" I will wait for him," she thought. " He could not possibly be here yet: he is not so eager as I am."

And she laughed a little trill into the desert air that had no terrors for her.

She sat on the pallet.

She sat on the druid's chair before his oaken table.

She sat on the table.

She jumped from it, and ran to the pallet, and lay on it on her back, holding her gleaming arms high above her head, and examining how they were white, how they were soft and tempting: seeing with the inward eye her whole body that would be given, utterly, ravidly; and that would be taken, gluttonously, utterly.

An impatience that was a veritable rage fell on her as in the blink of an eye.

She sat furiously on the pallet. She leaped furiously from it.

" That dog! " she cried.

225 Q

And her little mouth was suddenly one
that could bite, and her kind eyes were
daggers of flame.

"Let him die!" she hissed. "Let him
die a thousand times and be buried and
rot! . . . He makes me wait!"

Her mind trolled and rolled in a
remembered thunder.

"Am I the Queen or am I not? Am I
his butter-wench that he can faint at and
poke away in a hut . . .!"

She could have torn her clothes, her very
face.

But his face— She could have stripped
it in hot venom and cold venom, and pushed
his eyes in with her finger and picked them
out again with a pin. . . .

She heard a step without. Rage deserted
her as though it had never been. She panted
with hope, with expectation. . . .

Her face was one radiancy of smiling.
Her mind was meeker than a brooding
dove's. . . .

He should be pleased . . . how she
would please him . . .!

The step halted on the threshold. It
crossed the threshold. And, as she poised

226

like a soaring bird to meet him, she was suddenly unpoised and limp and thunderstruck, for it was not Ailill that entered.

CHAPTER XXXII

IT was a tall grave man who stood looking on her from his great height. He brooded on her in an absorption that astonished even while it reassured her. But that she would not run before a man, she should have fled to pick up her cloak, to hide away all that glimmering of hair and arms and neck, and all that shimmering of silk and silver.

She stood, and, but for a summoning of queenliness, she would have thought—" I am discovered." That thought lay on an horizon, unthought, but not unknown.

Meanwhile, he, who would not speak, that stranger, must be spoken to.

" Sir," she said, " how do you come here? "

" Etain! " said that stranger.

And he did not advance nor move, nor did he move even his eyes.

227

She put her hand to her brow, for suddenly she was teased by memory, and it told her in the one surging that she knew and did not know this man.   Her mind careered in her childhood, fled through her memories, and it told her that he was not there.

—And all this was in an instant, for not even the lightning is so speedy as the strung mind—

" I am Etain," she said.

" I have mourned for you," said that tall man.

But she looked at him with a blank astonishment.

" I am Midir," he said.

" I do not know you," said Etain.

He strode two great steps to her and halted.

" Once you knew me well."

" I have never known you," said Etain.

And again her hand fled to her forehead, for her mind had suddenly reproached her, and, as suddenly, had gone to sleep.

She was bewildered, and to escape that she fled into anger.

" Go!" she said. " It is not you I wait for."

A little smile curled the stranger's lip.

" The man you wait for was sent by me."
But she could only stare to hear this.

" And he was withheld from coming by me."

But Etain laughed scornfully at him.

" Are you from the Shí? " she mocked, and she would have passed him.

" I am Midir of the Shí," he said.

CHAPTER XXXIII

In its moments the mind can despise argument or explanation, and as a flower accepts rain, so it can accept a statement. It was so now with Etain's mind, and, on the utterance, she accepted its truth.

But no person has accepted truth without terror, and it was a pale girl that halted under Midir's arm, and that fled desperately from him, and that hunted for a way of escape.

There was no way, and she peered fearfully over her shoulder at the great man who had not moved.

" Are you afraid of me? " he asked, and there was astonishment in his tone.

But she made no reply: she but peered at him, lightly, palely.

"You were not frightened when you ran from me to Angus of the Brugh!"

And indeed Etain was frightened of him no more. She gave one high and trembling laugh, and faced him. She was now ashamed only that any person should have seen her frightened.

"In truth, sir," she said, "what a woman do you make me out! I have run from you to Angus, I have run from Angus to Eochaid, and I have run from Eochaid to Ailill. I can run no more."

And, at the words, as though some revelation had stripped her soul, she broke to a passion of tears, and felt that she, who had abandoned so much, and so many, was herself abandoned, and was utterly lost in a waste universe.

"Nay," said Midir, "it was only from me that you ran. It is only to me that you need return. Why did you fly from me, Etain?"

She wiped her tears on her silken gown.

"I am dreaming," she said, "or I have gone mad . . . Lord! have I truly gone mad? I cannot remember you."

And her lips twitched piteously, and with her soft arms she nursed herself, pitying the strayed babe that she knew herself to be.

" If you saw me as I am," said the stranger thoughtfully, " you might remember me. I will give you the eye of the gods."

He looked at her and moved two fingers, and Etain saw—

She saw might and majesty and beauty. She saw wonder—

Her mind leaped as in a flame, and she cried aloud:

" Fuamnach! Fuamnach! Fuamnach! "

" You remember! " said Midir.

" I wronged Fuamnach," cried Etain.

" She is dead," said Midir; " Angus took off her head."

" Oh! " said Etain.

But her mind could not hold, and it flagged away.

" Poor Fuamnach! " she sighed, " she was my friend.   When did she die? "

" By your time, eighteen years ago."

" And by yours? "

" Eighteen minutes ago."

" Eighteen minutes," she stammered.

" I have but strode from her body," said

Midir. "Angus could not think what to do. His bloody deed had unnerved him. But I caught that Bresil Etarlaim in my mind as one catches a pebble in his hand; and I emptied him of all that was in him as one empties a jug; and I followed you as an eagle swoops after a dove—and yet I am eighteen of your years too late . . .! These times are an endless trouble," said the god. "Had I come speedier I should have seen you as a babe, and as a growing girl. I should like to have seen you thus, Etain!"

"What did you do to this Bresil Etarlaim?" said wide-eyed Etain.

"I had no time to do anything but to empty him. But when I return I shall pick him from wherever he is hiding, and I shall blow him away as he blew you, and will blow him where he blew you."

"Did he blow me?"

"To this earth," said Midir.

"To Eochaid," said Etain.

Her eyes shone, and she ran to the great man: she laid a little hand upon his sleeve.

"You must not kill that Bresil," she coaxed.

CHAPTER XXXIV

"I MUST fly. I must run. I shall be missed, I——"

"Do not be troubled," said Midir. "There is no need for haste."

But Etain's mind assembled, reviewed, the ladies of her household, who had eyes and tongues.

"Indeed, there is every need for haste," she said decidedly.

"I have put all these people to sleep," said Midir. "There is not a person awake. There is not a dog awake within ten miles of Tara. Let us talk," he said. "We have all the time that we may need."

"Why," she demanded, "did you play all those tricks on Ailill?"

"I played them on you," he answered. "That young man has seemed to be sick a little: he has been a little in love, and already he has forgotten both of these adventures."

"He will never forget," said Etain.

"In truth he has never known what happened," said Midir.

"How do you say that?"

" He was not there.   It was I was in his body.   It was I that was sick, and I that was in love."

" And he," said Etain, " where, then, was he? "

" He was whistling somewhere on the wind," said Midir.   " It is of no consequence."

" But how do you say that it was to me you did these things? "

" It is simple.   You could not see me, you could not hear me.   Your mind had to be tormented and fevered and exalted before you could see a god."

" It was cruel of you to do this," she said.

" Was it so?   And yet, already, you have recovered, and already your mind can say —' it was only a game.'—Is there one ache left of all that pain? "

" There is no ache left," said Etain wonderingly; " it was only a wonderful game."

And she reviewed that strange fact, relieved that an irreparable evil had not come to pass, and strangely mournful that the wildest experience of her life had been based on, cored in, nothing.

" It was only a dream," she sighed.

" It was not a dream," said Midir; " it was a game."

" . . . It was unprofitable."

" You have not had to pay," he said, " and the adventure has been saved for you in your mind. Thus you have gained, and you will never be the same person again."

" Indeed, I never shall," she affirmed.

" And that is part of the eternal game," said Midir, " for all that is is only in a game."

" Perhaps . . .! " said Etain, with a little shiver. " But why have you come from the Shí? "

" I came for you. I have loved you for more than a thousand of these years, and you have forgotten me in eighteen miserable minutes. How strange," he went on, " are all these rememberings and forgettings and rememberings."

" I will not go with you," said Etain.

" You must," he said sternly, " for I shall take you. In a little while this place, this world, will be empty of you, and all these phantom people will scarcely remember you, and will never know you more."

" I too will remember," said Etain.

" Wherever you bring me I shall remember Eochaid, and I shall remember what you dared do to him, and to me."

She dashed tigerishly at him:

" By my hand!   Am I the Queen, or am I not? "

But Midir bent his brow into his hand.

" You are the Queen," he said.   " You will do your will; but some time your will and mine may be at one. . . ."

" Let me sing you a song," he entreated her.

" Why! " Etain exclaimed, confounded. " Certainly, you may sing me a song."

" It is the Death Song," said Midir.

The Queen shrank from him, white-cheeked, wide-eyed, panting:

" I will hear your song," she stammered, " but I shall not go with you."

" It is hard to resist the Death Song," he said.

" If I go with you, I shall remember," said Etain.   " But I shall not go with you."

She sat stubbornly on the pallet-bed, and, full of awe and curiosity and courage, she stared on the King from Faery.

" I shall not force you," said Great Midir,
" but I will sing you the song of my land.
When the mortal hears it he comes to my land.
He lets all fall: he makes no more delay."

" I will not go with you," said Etain.

CHAPTER XXXV

THERE was heard about Midir, and as it
were coming from him, a sound, as though a
small and very sweet bell were ringing at tiny
intervals; and in a moment this bell was
joined by others in faint pealings and
swingings and clashings.

" You hear? " said the god.

" The Bells! " said Etain. " So delicate!
So sweet! "

" They soothe," said Midir. " All those
about to die are soothed by the Bells. At
the moment when their torment is greatest
they pause to listen, and they know pain no
more: and, on the ceasing of the Bells, they
hear the Song."

" The Song of Death," she murmured.

" . . . And then they come away, away,

237

where pain or trouble may not stay, where all is great and good and gay, in the Wonderful Land."

"The Bells have ceased," said Etain.

"The Land of Music. The Land of Magic. The Wonderful Land.

"There the primrose blows and blossoms in the hair. Snow-white are the arms of the maidens there. Strong are the men, and wise and fair, in the Wonderful Land.

"Fair is the world in plain and hill. But sweeter far, and fairer still, each vale and mead and wood and rill of the Wonderful Land.

"Will you, can you still delay? Grey and gloom are gone to-day. The world is gone, away, away, to the Wonderful Land. . . ."

But the Queen was not listening.

Her eyes were closed that she might not see Midir. Her fingers were thrust in her ears that she might not hear him, and yet, through her clogged senses, peace would invade her.

It was not lassitude, it was abnegation that assailed her. She wished, did she not will, to cease from all of labour, from all of difficulty. To lose all that she was, and all that she had known.

Her mind beat about its prison as a wild bird flies and beats within a cage. . . .

What was she that was worth being? Had she aught that was worth the keeping? What did she know that was worthy of knowledge? Was there in the world but foolishness in being and in knowing? To rise in the morning and to sleep in the night! and between these to engage in futilities of thought and deed and emotion!

Almost she had lapsed to Midir, all but she was gone with him, when her heart sang, cleanly, sweetly, innocently:

"—My Branch! My Love! My Bird! My Lamb! Though all but seem, though all be sham, he is my Bird, my Love, my Lamb!

" My Land of Wonder and Delight! My Sun by day, my Moon by night! My Darkness and my Lovely Light!

" My Dream and my Awakening! My Treasure and my Song I sing! My Love, my Life, my Everything! "

She took her fingers from her ears. She opened her eyes and opposed the god with

a radiant brow. But already he had ceased
from that chaunting, and, with his face bowed
to his hand, he sat in silence.

He raised his head.
" I have not forced you," said Midir.
" You could not."
But he smiled gravely at the lovely Queen:
" It would be so easy for me! It would
be so much easier to do than to undo—You
will come to me yet."
" I shall not."
" This High King will give you to me."
" It is unthinkable."
" If he gave you to me? "
" He could not."
" If he did? "
But she grew gentle at his persistence:
" If it comforts you to dream a foolish
dream——"
" If he gave you to me, you would come
to me? "
" There might be nothing else to do,"
said Etain.
Midir stood from his chair. He strode
to the door. He disappeared in the dark-
ness, and his footsteps echoed away.

240

In a moment Etain went after him. She
returned to the palace, and to a bed that was
radiant with vision, and terrible with dream.

CHAPTER XXXVI

" AND this Lord of the Shí? " said Eochaid.

" He was wonderful," she cried. " He
was very marvellous."

" By my hand! I should like to have seen
that man."

" He showed himself to me in his god-
form."

" Ah! "

" He could have plucked down clouds.
His hair was all a-whistling of golden flame.
His eyes were bright as sunlight. He was
more powerful than a winter storm, and
gentler than a flower. He could not be
looked at for more than an instant. He was
a blazing, blinding loveliness."

" Of what Shí was he? "

" I have forgotten! Indeed, I have forgotten even his name."

" Try to remember it," he urged. " We

must protect ourselves against this god if he comes again; and if we had his name we should know what to expect."

" I cannot remember."

" If I but had his name," Eochaid pondered. " My caste, my station, my office knows all that is to be known about the gods. We are at peace with them. But if I had his name we should guess how he might move, and, even, that he would or would not move.

" For," he explained, " some of the People of Dana are full of whim and fantasy, and will turn aside at just the sound of laughter, or a noise; and others move steadily, doing for ever all that they imagine."

" . . . I must go into the Shí," he said thoughtfully.

" You must not dream——! " said Etain, appalled. " You must not dare——! "

" I am crowned Monarch and Magician," said Eochaid.

He smiled at his trembling wife.

" The High King of Ireland is master of two arts," he said. " Listen, it will be simple——"

" Nay, it will be deadly."

" It will be quite simple. I shall go to some of the lesser gods and get their advice, even their help. I can ask for advice from Bove of Shí Femen, or Midir of Bri Leith, or from Ethal Anbual of the Western Shí. I could even go to Angus of the Brugh. But Midir or Bove will love to help the High King."

"Do nothing whatever," said Etain. " It was just a whimsy of that god. He came to play a trick on you and on your brother, and on me. He had, perhaps, a wager that it could be done, and since he got home he has found ten girls to play with, or one, perhaps, that suits him."

" They can behave just like little boys," said Eochaid. " They are delightful."

" Was it not a mean trick? "

" It was. By my hand, it was a vulgar trick! I cannot think of one Lord of Faery that would stoop to it. It should have been some pupil out on a wild adventure, and probably quaking now at the very memory of his daring."

" In this case, if it had happened," said Etain timidly. " It did not happen, you

243

understand—but, if it had happened, should I have been terribly wrong? Would you have been dreadfully angry if I had done what I intended to do for Ailill?"

"It could not have happened," said Eochaid.

He laid a great arm about his wife. Her blushes went into hiding on his shoulder, and a great tremor ran from her heart to his.

"If it had been done," she sobbed, "it would still have been done for you."

"It could not have been done," said the King, in a voice of stone.

"It could," she stammered.

"If it had been done," said Eochaid, "it would have been done as a queen should do it."

There came a long silence between them.

"My Lamb!" said Etain timidly.

"My Dove!" said Eochaid.

"I love you," said Etain.

"Do you truly love me?" said Eochaid.

"I do, I do," she replied.

"In what way?" said Eochaid, and he was all intentness and anguish.

The Queen drew a great breath into her lungs, and she breathed it deeply abroad.

244

" Thus," she said, and she beat mightily on her lovely bosom.

" . . . Indeed, you must not cry," said Eochaid. " Indeed, you will make me cry," he said.

CHAPTER XXXVII

LIFE took up its accustomed round, and in a little the King could consider that nothing of note had happened in the past, and that the days and nights to come would not greatly differ from those he now enjoyed.

But something had happened.

In the normal case, to lose fear is almost to have gained knowledge; and to lose a memory that is painful is a ripened event. But to lose a memory ere its work is done is a misfortune. These two had forgotten the sting that should have been in their memory, and had lost the fear that sting would have kept alive.

Fear is the wisdom of ignorance; it is its safeguard also. For when we fear we go cautiously; we scan abroad and behind us

ere we venture; and we ponder ourselves
and all about us, and so grow wise, grow
fearless.

But if Etain and Eochaid had forgotten,
Midir had not; and if they were careless
it was because his care made them so.

His territories in the Shí were in no
danger. Fuamnach was dead—was, that is,
vanished from his sphere, and, except for
his duties to his overlords, Angus and the
Dagda, he could afford to be absent from
his kingdom long enough, or at long enough
intervals, to do what he should plan.

He would plan.

It was one thing that Angus Óg of the
Brugh should take his wife from him—
such a matter ran in rights and customs
and prerogatives which his own exalted
position bound him to respect and participate
in. He had suffered a loss, but not an evil,
and, certainly, he had submitted to no
indignity.

It was quite different that a mortal should
do this.

That this mortal was the High King
of Ireland did modify his thoughts on the
matter. The High King of Ireland, by

breeding once, and once again by his great office, is twice a god, and Midir could allow that, technically, no insult had been given or received. He could, therefore, regard Eochaid without anger; and could contemplate the relation between the High King and Etain without jealousy. Jealousy, in fact, has nothing to do with sex. It is purely egoistic.

He was spared those pangs.

But he was not prepared to allow this condition to continue.

The High King of another country has privileges but not rights in another country. Eochaid was an Over-Lord in the earth. Midir was a Lord in the Shí. The distinction, touching prerogatives, was plain.

But more! Etain although in the earth, and unable to leave the earth, was not of the earth. She did not belong there. She belonged to the Shí. She had not died in the Shí. She had been forcibly and criminally emigrated from her world. She had not been dead even for an instant, and she was, therefore, not only a lawful subject of the Dagda. She was Midir's wife; and his claim to her was not and could not be abrogated by any heavenly or earthly law, or by any interplanetary event or accident.

His case was so unanswerable that, had he submitted to judgement at Tara, Eochaid would have been bound to admit his facts and to render him their wife.

But Midir loved " the long-limbed, winsome lady."

He would not have minded that the nobles of two worlds should know her history—there is no scandal in exalted knowledge; but that she should become a tale for the camps and guest-houses of earth did not please him; and, in terms of her honour, could not be tolerated.

He cast about to see how he might regain his wife; and, as those who can think are happy while they are thinking, he was not unhappy.

CHAPTER XXXVIII

THE Games were being played at Tara.

It was the Feast of Gracious Commemoration, of Lugh, and of the Great Queen Taillte.

At the Fort of the Synod the law-makers

were deliberating on such changes as were politic, and discussing recent events that could modify procedure, or be considered as new, or overriding, precedents. Their bards, who, for the sake of easy memory, had " put a thread of rhyme about the laws," were in attendance, and were considering the metrical surgery that any change in the body of law made necessary.

The bards were in Convention at the Well of the Elf Mound discussing if all that could be achieved by the Great Eight-Line Curved Verse could not be as competently managed by the Little Eight-Line Curved Verse, and whether the Great-Curving Eight-Line Return Verse was a necessity or an outrage: these holding that brevity, and those that diversity, was the chief ornament of poetry.

" Where there is only room for brevity," quoth a young bard, " there is no room for poetry."

A savage ancient confounded him.

" Where, sir, there is space for diversity there is place and to spare for foolishness."

" A goat in a small plot," cried a pastoral bard, " starvation follows."

"Ah!" cried another, who knew his animals, "a goat in a large plot—extended destruction!"

Love poems, war poems, place poems, histories—this would be a busy, a contentious, gathering.

Some additions to the rules governing chess had to be considered, for the High King happened also to be the Champion Chess player of Ireland, and he had made suggestions which chess-players debated with abhorrence and with enthusiasm.

The participation of women and poets in war was becoming an angrily debated question. Those arguing that women should not be permitted to fight and that poets should not be allowed to be killed; and these others responding that women and poets and every other person should have part in the common risk as they had part in the common security of their land.

"But that question," said Maeve, " was not settled until my father succeeded Eochaid Airem in the throne, for it was he that settled it; and, as he loved women and poets, he settled it in terms of their security."

The Provincial Kings had each a palace

allotted to him, and were housed there with
their queens, their Tanists, their druids,
their councillors and courtiers; and these
vied with each other in the splendour of
their retinues, the gaiety of their hearts, and
their liberality to the populace.

Nigh the Rampart of the Three Whispers
the chief Physicians were debating their
craft—explaining how this man had died in
despite of such or such a treatment; and
how, by the administration of this herb, unused before, a cure had been effected.

The master-brewers, in session at the
Mound of the Hostages, were telling of the
difference that ten minutes or two minutes
of heat made in the brew, and of how the
waters of such a locality made an excellent
or a detestable liquor.

Close to the Stones of the Three Wizards,
each with his reverent audience, were the lesser
story-tellers with tales of sacks and forays and
wooings; tales of deaths and demons; tales
of tabu, of valour, of comedy, and of lust.

There were those, at the Well of the
Dark Eyes, who would teach you ten new
proverbs for a farthing; and their rivals who
would sell you three powerful incantations

for a penny.   Three lines of verse against
the rheumatism; six couplets that will kill
a witch; or a sovereign ten-lined verse to
mend a toothache.

On the Slope of the Chariots there were
men of lesser medicine who would dis-
possess one's soul of a devil, or one's toe of
a corn, at a price that had never before been
heard of.

There were pipers and fiddlers and gleemen; and there were merry monsters who
clicked miracles out of bones, so that every
one who heard them went mad and danced
until they dropped.

If you went yonder, out on the Moor of
Tara, you could see a red mouth hedged
deeply with whiskers, and from among these
a ballad is roared that will roast you to
death in your own blushes, or reduce you
to such a jelly of laughter that you cannot
protect your purse or your hat from the
skilful family of the singer.

Yonder, in the leathern cap, will fight
three rounds with a wolf-hound, if the fee is
made up:

" Nothing but teeth to be used, nobles,
nothing but teeth."

He, with the bells in his ears, will eat three feet of a spear, and enjoy them.

Behind him is one that can swallow a fathom of flaming tow; and beyond again is one who will crunch broken crockery and devour it into the stomach that God gave him, for a small recompense.

The master wood-workers, house-builders, sword-makers, horse- and cow-breeders were there, as were those who dealt in every comestible and contrivance and contraption that could be thought of: and everywhere the slaves, bearing the tonsure of servitude, were flying on the businesses of their masters, with a "By your leave, gentles. By your good leave, all."

Indeed the pick of all Ireland were there, "to bewail kings and queens, to lament revenges and ill-deeds," and to be merry when memory was served; and they were fed and entertained by the High King, each according to his rank or craft or excellence.

In the fields about Tara the games for all those who had died in the past three years were being played; for the Feast of Lugnasa and the National Games were then as now, held at three-yearly intervals, and were played by the champions of the yearly local games.

The first week's games were in honour of the Gods and the dead, the second in honour of the High King, the third and fourth weeks were divided into so many days, each in honour of the Women, in honour of the Guardians, in honour of the Princes, in honour of the Craftsmen, and in honour of the Populace.

Eochaid had appeared at every gathering, and had been acclaimed and adored. But after some time, when, with Etain, he had crowned the Victors of the Games, and grew weary of the throng, he would go to the great flat roof of his palace, that was thatched or carpeted through its entirety with birds' wings—the rook, the heron, the eagle, the gull, the swan—there was no bird but a dozen of his wings were there, a marvellous mosaic and incrustation of shade and shape and colour. From thence he could see in every direction, thirty miles in the round; and he could examine from the height all that was astir, and the Fair rich with streamers, with chariots, and with mettled horses.

254

He could hear, thinned by the height, the rolling, the rattling, the booming of the drums; the trumpets calling out the time; the fiddles calling out the dance; the hollow-throated horns calling echoes from the woods; the pipes calling to pride and danger; and the timpan telling unweariedly of love.

He was standing so, on the Day of the Populace, the last day of the Games, when he saw, far out on the plain, a chariot driving at all speed to Tara, and the speed and excellence of the driving so took his eye that he watched its approach, idly, but speculatively; for man nor king can see unmoved the coming of a wind-filled sail, the coming of a lovely lady, the coming of a horse in speed.

He called to his herald:

" Whom do we expect? "

The herald recited a list of those who were due to arrive.

" Yonder chariot is not any of these," said the King. " If its lord asks audience, let him be brought here. I should like to know more about his horses and their training."

CHAPTER XXXIX

THE herald returned precipitately.

" Majesty," he stammered, " this lord bears a weapon."

" What! Does he not know that during the month Lugnasa no arms can be borne by a loyal subject? "

" He bears a shield, too, Majesty."

" Ha! What is its device? "

" It has none, sir. It is a silver shield with golden knobs on it."

" I do not remember that shield," said Eochaid, " because I can recollect two dozen of it. What is his name? "

" He will not say, sir. He will only say that he bears a challenge."

" By my hand! I am a challengeable man. Send me that stranger."

The stranger was brought; a tall man, with golden hair and shining blue eyes. He was dressed in a purple cloak with golden fringes that danced and swung to his robust stride.

The King watched him narrowly, and spurted upon him sudden and emphatic words:

256

" Do you come straight from barbarism? Do you not know that during the Grand Féis no arms can be carried ? "

" Majesty," said the stranger, " I brought my weapons by simple bad habit. I am so used to carrying them that my hand seized on them forgetfully, and I was so anxious to deliver my challenge——"

" Do you not know that during the Féis Lugnasa and the Games no challenge can be given by any man nor accepted by any man? "

" It is a peaceful challenge, Majesty."

" I have never heard of a peaceful challenge," said Eochaid testily; " these words do not consort."

" It is merely a challenge to the Champion Chess player of Ireland——"

" Oh! " said Eochaid, and he sat all up and all round, staring at the stranger.

" Can you beat me? " he demanded.

" I can, Majesty."

" I do not believe it."

" The proof is not difficult," the stranger insinuated.

" It truly will not be difficult," said the King.

And, now, he was weighing and cogitating this robust opponent.

" The challenger calls the game," he said, " but the Champion names the stakes."

" That will suit me," the other agreed.

Eochaid waved to the herald.

" My board."

" The Queen has it," said the herald.

" Mine may do? " the stranger suggested.

He brought a chess board from beneath his cloak.

" It is of old silver," said Eochaid.   " I like those stones in the corners."

He examined the golden pieces that were shaken from a bag of shining gold thread.

" These are as good as my own.   I shall ask for your craftsman's name; and you must tell me who put the axle into your chariot, and who it is that trains your horses? "

" Good men all, Majesty," said the stranger.   " Very good men."

He bowed to the King enquiringly, and the King's eager hand permitted him to be seated.

" Majesty," said the stranger, " shall we name the stakes? "

"When the game is won," Eochaid answered. "The winner will name the stakes."

"It will make the game more exciting," the stranger assented thoughtfully. "Will a revenge game be permitted?"

"Certainly," said the King, "and thus there will be two winnings for some one."

CHAPTER XL

THEY began to play, and during the first few moves Eochaid was as much engaged in studying his opponent as he was in studying his opponent's game.

There were things he would leave to chance, for he was deeply enamoured of that wanton goddess; but a move in a game of chess was something that he would not entrust to her, for though he credited her with all good intentions towards himself, he did not believe that she could play chess as well as he could.

The stranger made a move, casual in appearance, but Eochaid caught the blue

259

glint of an hostile eye darting from that bent face.

He leaned back in his chair, and solemnly studied the board.

" Thus," he said, and his upraised finger adjudged a movement that his mind contemplated.

" And thus," he said, and his finger pondered the next consequence of that move.

" And thus," he murmured encouragingly.   " And then! " he thundered; and his finger darted in upon itself, and ended a cogitation.

But he did not yet make his move.   He regarded his opponent, and addressed that hidden mind with his other hand and a quite different finger.

" Whereupon? " he inquired, and his finger remained stationary.

" And thereupon! " he continued, and he waggled that finger solemnly and threateningly.

" And thereafter! " the stranger mused contentedly, and he did not move a finger at all.

" Thereafter is very distant," said Eochaid. " Do you go easily to ' thereafter '? "

" Not easily, perhaps, but I think I know where ' thereafter ' goes to bed."

" I think I know too," said Eochaid, and his eyes went back to the board, and thence to his hand.

He addressed his hovering thumb and first finger:

" You have played this move an hundred times," he said, " and I have always said to you, ' Think well before you touch the piece.'

" It seems clear," he said to his thumb, " but the fog crawls over the mountain in a minute.

" It seems sound," he admonished his first finger, " but so does the top of a bog.

" I will make my move "—and his obedient first two digits, as though they impended on an ox, lifted weightily that piece—" thus," he said.

And the piece was scrupulously planted, and released with precaution.

" And I," said the stranger, moving his diligent brow and thumb in unison, " will follow you in—this manner."

" Whereupon," said Eochaid, and he detached and deposited a hill.

"And thereupon," said the stranger briskly.

"And thereafter," said Eochaid, in the voice of one who mourns at his mother's tomb—

He waved a sad hand to the figure of some one, lord, herald, fosterling, who was staring nigh.

"Bring two large, strong, restoring drinks for the players," he said gloomily.

"You have not moved!" he enquired. "Nay," and he smiled tenderly on the stranger. "You hesitate to slay your prince. And yet, if die I must, it is here that I must die."

"I shall move in a minute," the other replied gruffly.

The King stared in doubt and consternation on the board:

"I love a cautious player," he said, and his convulsed and constricted inwards impelled sounds from his nose that were due to the pangs of death or of laughter.

He seized his goblet and buried himself therein as though he would evade doom in the dregs of the cup. He addressed the jewel that was set in the bottom of the vessel.

" Do not mock me," he said deeply.   " Do not twinkle at a ruined man.

" Give that drink to this lord," he commanded to the hands that would have replenished his goblet.

But the stranger waved the offering aside, and moistened his lips with his own fevered tongue.

Eochaid leaned to the board and examined it intently.

" I am wondering," he said, " what crafty move you will loose upon me now."

But the stranger looked at him stonily.

" I cannot move," he growled.

" By my hand! " said Eochaid in a tone of great astonishment.

He gaped on the stranger and on the board.

" By my hand! " he roared, " I should like to see you try to move."

And he loosed a mighty laughter that drowned the laughter and applause of the onlookers.

CHAPTER XLI

"The stakes," said the stranger coldly and briefly.

"You may give me," said Eochaid thoughtfully—"you may give me fifty such horses as those you have below.   The horses below shall be two of the fifty."

"I have not got fifty," said the stranger.

"It is a pity," Eochaid replied.   "You can, perhaps, find the horses you lack elsewhere?"

"There are no such horses in the world, sir."

"Alas!" said Eochaid, "I must then be satisfied with all the horses that you have got."

The stranger's face was composed, but his hands showed something of the agitation he would conceal.

"You shall have the horses," he said, "within the week."

"Could I not have them to-morrow?" said Eochaid.

"It can be managed," said the stranger.

"I will lend you——" said Eochaid,

264

" I will give you two horses to get home with."

The stranger rose to his feet, but he could no longer restrain his feelings, and, in the act of rising, he so far forgot himself as to beat his fist on the table.

" I claim the game of revenge," he growled.

The King looked at him with open eyes.

" Are you wise to claim this game? " he asked kindly.

" I know that I can win," the stranger cried.

" You know nothing of the kind."

" I know the very place I lost," the other returned in great excitement. " I had a moment's inexplainable forgetfulness. Your fingers, and your talk to your fingers, distracted me. It is a trick."

" But I could not play," the King expostulated, " if I did not talk to my fingers. You know, every player knows, that when the game grows great the mind goes into a trance, and it is the fingers that play."

" I know that I can beat you," said the stranger, " and I know that you promised me the game of revenge."

And on the word the stranger stamped violently on delicate and lovely plumage that was not meant to be tramped on.   The King observed the violence of his gesture and of his feet with the stern self-restraint of an outraged host—

"You shall have your game," he said coldly.

The man sat instantly.

"The stakes, Lord?" he said.

"They shall be named by the winner."

"The winner will pay?" said the stranger savagely.

But Eochaid looked on him in a rage and a disdain that was all ice and lightning.

"Do you doubt that the King will pay?"

"I doubt everything.   You have taken my horses."

"It was fair," said Eochaid.

"You say the winner must name the stakes.   Will my stake be paid if I win?"

"Get to this game," said Eochaid.   "If you can win it you will be paid whatever you can ask, except my kingdom."

"There are exceptions," the stranger sneered.

"It is the only one," said Eochaid.

266

CHAPTER XLII

THE pieces were set, and again the players looked on each other before the first move was made; but this was a different look to that they had before exchanged. It was a look of frank hatred: cold on the part of Eochaid, blustering and fevered on the part of the stranger. Eochaid's eyes dwelt on the great masculine face, and dropped from it to the mighty shoulders and the vast breast below.

Here was a man huge as Eochaid himself —" but not so quick," his mind murmured. —For a joyous instant he saw that bulk confronting his, and between himself and that man the sparkle and flash of two wise swords.

The King's Champion who stood beside, and who, in matters such as this, could read the King's mind as he could read his own, bent to Eochaid—

" Sir," he said, " that would be my prerogative."

But the stranger had followed the short silence, and that short sentence. He leaned back in his chair, and his hands were clapped heavily on his thighs, as, with a violent eye and mouth, he stared at and addressed the Champion—

" You do not love your life! " he snarled.

" By my soul I do," the Champion returned, " and I am trained to take care of it."

But the stranger smiled grimly, and turned an eye measuringly on the King.   He jerked a vulgar thumb at the Champion.

" Majesty," he said, " when I had fed my dogs with the King's Champion——"

But Eochaid laughed loud and long.

" No! No! " he cried, " you cannot do it that way, my friend."

" What can I not do? "

" You cannot make me angry and spoil my game.   You almost managed it.   Those uncomely manners are not natural to you."

The stranger then looked frankly and nobly at the King.

" Majesty," he said, " I shall anger you at the close of this game."

" I will forgive you in advance," cried Eochaid.

" I shall love you if you can," said the stranger, with a curious stern kindness.

Eochaid placed his hand on a piece.

" Those dogs you spoke of——" he said thoughtfully.

" Yes," the stranger murmured, following intently the move.

" I may be interested in them at the end of this game," said Eochaid.

The stranger deliberated on his piece and made his move.

" They are good dogs," he murmured.

Eochaid's finger was sternly upraised, and was being severely frowned on ere it fell to the board.

" They would surely be good dogs," he assented.

" Yes," said the pondering stranger, and he edged his piece gently to the new position.

" They have perhaps been trained with your horses—my horses, I mean? "

" They eat together, hunt together, sleep together."

" Ah! " said Eochaid, following deeply the consequences of that last move.

" You are playing a better game this time," he mused, and he took two pieces from his opponent.

" I think I am," said the stranger, and he too deliberated his move.

269

"About these dogs," he murmured, and he placed a finger-tip on a piece, and removed it again, reluctantly.

"About these dogs, even if I lose this game I shall make a present of them to your Majesty."

Eochaid looked at him then directly, approvingly, kindly.

"I will match your present by only accepting half of them, and by giving you a present of half of your own horses. What was your move that time? I see."

"There will be two great kennels in Ireland," said the stranger.

"We shall challenge each other," cried Eochaid gleefully. "Horse races, chariot races, hounds——"

"And they can run," said the stranger.

"Oh!" said Eochaid.

"What is it, Majesty?"

The stranger's face was cold, his lips were stern, and his eyes were piercing. And at him also Eochaid stared, as it were two mountains of granite lowering upon one another.

"You could not make me angry," said Eochaid.

" I could not."

" So you made me affectionate! "

The stranger uttered not a word.

" It was a woman's trick," said Eochaid.

" I had to win this game or die," said the stranger.

Eochaid bent his master-mind on the board, and saw all that had occurred.

" There it began," he grumbled, " and in that silly way it was done."

He was transfixed with disgust and astonishment, and could have fallen to a very desolation, but that his eye fell on the Herald and the Champion and the lords who stood about, and the bewilderment that he saw on those faces so tickled him that he fell to a mighty laughter from which he could not quickly recover himself.

CHAPTER XLIII

HE strode to the stranger, who rose to meet him. He thudded a great hand on that man's shoulder and rocked him where he stood.

271

" You have won," he said. " It is the first time and the last time of your life that you will beat the King. What is your stake? "

The stranger murmured in his ear.

The King stared at him, and then leaped from him as though he had been pricked by a sword.

" What! " he said.

And then in a whisper of dreadful ire:

" If you truly said those words, say them again."

" Will you not bid these people depart? " said the stranger.

" They shall stay," cried Eochaid. " Name aloud your stake."

And his terrible eyes dared the man to do so. But the stranger turned on him a brow as royal and a stare as terrific.

" I claim the King's wife, Etain, as my stake," he thundered.

Those who were present bounded in their places. The King's hand darted to his side, but no sword was hanging there. His Champion swung his shoulders as one who heaves a shield around, and his right hand gripped where the axe should swing. But he bore neither shield nor axe. He and all in the kingdom were disarmed for the Games, and they would none of them be armed again until the next day. But the Champion shook two savage paws before the King.

"Let me kill him with these," he implored.

But the King did not answer him; did not hear him. He was lost in a trance of rage and hate of the man he stared at. His breast could scarcely find air, and his eyes could not stare enough at that man; to whom, moving as it were by the eyes and not by the feet, he stealthily advanced.

But the stranger did not look at him: he looked at the Champion.

"Stand hither," he said, in a roar of such command that the Champion did his bidding hastily and almost automatically. The stranger placed his hand on the man's shoulder, and under that pressure the Champion crumpled to the earth as though a roof had tumbled on him.

He came again to his feet, shaking and ashen-faced.

"With an axe in my hand——!" he stammered.

" With an axe in mine——! " said the stranger. And his grim smile played on and daunted the Champion.

Even the King was halted by the imperturbable force and the dauntless insolence of that man: but with an effort he drew his mind to attention. He banished all else and became a king, a plotter.

" Sir," he said, " is not this a wild jest, and has not the time come to end it? "

" It is not a jest."

" And you demand this stake!"

" I demand your wife."

" I will forgive you," said the King—" I will forgive you the forfeit I won, your beautiful horses."

" I will not accept that forgiveness."

" I will give up to you the Championship of Ireland."

" I have won it," the other replied; " you offer me nothing."

" To be haughty with a king and to be a fool are not two things," said Eochaid sternly.

" The king that wins well and does not lose well . . ." the stranger sneered.

But Eochaid was brooding on him coldly, murderously.

" We shall pay our debt," he said, " when you have paid yours."

" Ha! " said the stranger. " My horses shall be delivered to-morrow."

" I shall deliver my stake to you to-morrow," said Eochaid. " You are dismissed."

The stranger bowed before the King.

" Does your Majesty's promise of two horses to take me home still stand? "

Eochaid turned to his Herald.

" See that this gentleman has free choice in our stables."

CHAPTER XLIV

" BUT—" said Etain, halting between tears of rage and of laughter—" but this cannot be done."

" It certainly cannot," the King assented heartily.

" I should hope——"

" And yet," the King brooded, " I don't quite see how it is not to be done."

" What! "

" If that — person holds me to the
wager——"

" Am I the Queen, or am I not?" Etain
exploded. " What person can win me or
lose me in a wager! Ha!" said Etain.

" By my hand," said the King, " that is
truth and law. I can give him his wager,
but, if you do not agree to go with him,
he cannot accept it." And he thundered an
" Ha!" at Fate and Chance and Calamity.

" He is overreached!" said Eochaid.

He arose and trod the room briskly,
smiting various portions of himself with an
enthusiasm that would have crippled any
other man.

" I shall remit his wager," he said joyfully.
" I shall concede him the Championship, and
challenge him to another game to get it back.
I can beat him easily. I shall give him an
office in my own household, and will be good
to him in an hundred ways. I shall reward
that man until he follows me like a pet dog,
and I shall woo him until he yearns to die
for me. Ha! I am the King; I know men!"

He whirled on the transfigured Queen.

" There does not live the man that will
not love me."

" It is true," said Etain.

" Look! " he said, " I set myself, so. I forefront and confront that person; and, what is called for, be it guile or rage or affection, it arises spontaneously within me."

" It is exactly true," said Etain.

" There awakens within me a royal magnificence, a splendour that cannot be supported or evaded."

" It is precisely so," cried Etain. " But ——" and she went staring and silent.

" What is it, my Dove?"

" That man," said Etain, " did confront and did support——"

" He was upheld by the desire to win his game."

" He was bold enough—callous enough, to name a stake——"

" He was wild by an unexpected victory."

" He was steady enough to sneer as he departed, and rugged enough to smash the King's Champion to the ground in the very presence of the King."

" He——" said Eochaid.

" And in the very period of Lugnasa, and of the Féis! "

" In good truth," said Eochaid, " these

are considerable achievements, and this is
certainly a man to be thought of with some
care."

" I begin to be afraid of him," she said.

" I examine my soul," said Eochaid, " and
I say that I do not find any fear of him there.
We were face to face, brow to brow, will to
will, but I did not imagine for an instant
that he was my superior, nor at all my equal.
He is a nobly great personage, but, by my
hand, whether in guile or power, he could
never withstand me."

" He will come to-morrow," she whispered.

" He may not."

" He will surely come."

" He shall never return if he comes."

" Would you kill him? " she gasped.

" He has insulted the High King.   He
shall die as certainly as he comes.   And if
he does not come he shall, nevertheless,
die."

" But——" she sobbed, running to
him——

" Had this been a wild person, outrage-
ously wagering, I should have laughed and
forgiven him.   But you have proved that he
is a man of power and magnificence.   He

278

has not challenged me to a game. He has challenged the might of Ireland, and Ireland will kill him."

" No——" she implored.

" To-morrow," said Eochaid, " he shall be trampled to a bloody dirt."

CHAPTER XLV

THE morrow came, and arms were seen again in Ireland. Indeed few others than armed men were seen anywhere in the royal precincts.

Urgent orders had been issued, and during the night a vast evacuation had taken place.

The four great roads of Ireland met at Tara as at a common centre, and away on all of these roads, and away on all of their branches, the King's guests, the champions of the Games, the lawyers and poets, the doctors, the showmen, bread-vendors, apple-sellers, maltsters, pipers, fiddlers, gleemen, bone-players, ballad-singers, acrobats, pell-mell were streaming, were screaming, were grumbling, and yelling, and cursing; with, before and behind each troop of them, a squad of soldiers to disentangle the traffic and to keep all moving.

"What a work!" cried an exasperated officer, who was so powdered with dust and sweat that he seemed but a pillar of mud.

"Move thy damned mare!" he roared.

"She is in foal, master."

"Carry her, bosthoon!"

"Mother, if thou wilt not trot at more than a mile a week we shall fork thee on thine own bull's back and pitch rocks at the pair of ye."

"What now! what now!"

"The wheel is off my cart! The good new wheel!"

"Heave that cart to the ditch. Away with thee: fly with thy colt, thou confounded man!"

"Sheep! Hens! Oh Lord of the Elements! may I never herd hens again!"

"Look, thou cranky lout, if but one more pig of thy pigs run but once more backwards I shall make of him pork and of thee sausage-meat."

" Bees! Now God preserve me! And must they go so slowly? "

" If they go quicker, master, the hives will topple."

" Thy bees can fly home, can they not? thou slow beeman! "

" They can sting, master! "

" Until Doom, this night and hell will not seem different to me. Go gently, bee-man: keep thy warriors in their fortress——"

" Unhorn me those ten cows."

" Heave me this wreck to the ditch."

" Tie me a thistle to yon foal's tail."

" Clout me that pig."

" Gather me this hen off my helmet."

" Loosen me this goat from between my legs."

" Oh! hath any man a drink upon him! "

Ere the morning was advanced, for ten miles in the round, Tara was a desert; and, distantly, in the top of every tree, a soldier's bronzed helmet was glistering in the sun, and his eyes were scanning, distantly, anxiously, for a cloud of dust that he was told to expect and to give notice of.

Riders were dashing to all of these outposts with orders, and others were speeding to yet further stations on the great plain, halting their frothing steeds for an instant to give and to ask for news, and to exchange rumour.

" Why is it? What is the meaning of this burley? " cried a leathern-coated horseman.

" Ask me indeed! " said the slingsman he enquired of. " I can give you an hundred answers, and the devil knows if one of them is right. 'Tis a cattle plague, and a fire, and a raid from Leinster, and a Hosting of the Shí, and the Queen's family that is expected, and two thousand and ten seventies of pretty girls coming to look at the King."

" Whatever it is," said the horseman, drawing round on his bridle, " I'll be skinned and boiled if I'm half a minute late to my post."

" And I," said the slinger, drawing on his belt, " will be sliced and skewered if I'm half as late as that. Health, comrade, and run for it! "

CHAPTER XLVI

A YOUNG captain on his first service was
striding about a great tree. Seven of his
men were sprawling in the grass, and three
more were squatting in the tree-top. He
had sent one up to look out, and a second to
watch that the first was looking, and the
third to see that neither of these went to
sleep.

He drew his unused sword, unslung his
shield, and did some shadow fighting.

" Hither! " he called to the sprawlers.
" Hither, a man of you, and breath me! We
may have bloody work to-day."

A veteran loped forward, grinning.

" Have at me warmly," cried the young
officer.

" Warmly it is, master," the veteran
simpered, and he fetched his captain a crack
on the skull with his butt that sent the lad
down with his nose in the daisies and his legs
in the air. He scrambled to his feet, dropped
spear and shield, and went for the veteran
with his bare hands, and that so savagely that
the soldier ran for his life.

283

The veteran came warily back:

" Master," he said ingratiatingly.

" What is it? " said the fierce lad.

" What duty are we on, master? "

" A cloud of dust that may come from any direction.   A troop of horses that is raising that dust, and a lord riding among them that the King wants brought to him as tenderly as a hen carries an egg."

" There will be no fight to-day," said the glum soldier.

" If he has a troop we fight.   If he is alone we escort him; and, as we march, all troops fall in behind the escort.   He will come to the palace with a tail of five thousand men."

" By my wife's ten tongues! " quoth the amazed soldier.

" That gentle will have a tall tail! " said a staring comrade.

" And then," the young officer continued, for he was proud to have such news to relate, " when this noble enters the palace a file of twenty troops will be placed on every door; and behind each file, all around the palace gates, at an interval of fifty yards, there will be a squad of troops standing to arms; and behind them, and behind those again, and yet again to the very fortifications, and abroad beyond them, squad after squad of troops will be standing to arms."

The soldiers were grouped about him, gaping and wonderstruck. Quoth one:

" Is it the devil that is expected? "

" What will they stand to arms for? " the bemused veteran enquired.

" If," the captain replied—" if this gentleman that we are looking for comes out of a palace door alone he shall receive a military salute from the whole army, and shall be escorted with full honours to wherever he wishes to go."

" 'Tis unheard of! Is he a king, or a king's son? "

The captain raised his finger and imposed silence on his troop:

" If this gentleman comes out of the palace accompanied by a lady, even if that lady be the Queen herself, all troops will march instantly upon him, and will trample him to death."

" What! "

The young captain's face went pale as snow.

" Troops shall use no arms on this

gentleman. They shall trample him to death with their boots."

The veteran moistened a lip that had no particle of colour in it. He turned a sallow-grey face from the captain to his comrades.

" By the soul of my gods! " he stammered, " I hope that gentleman does not come our way."

" I hope that he does not come at all," said his young captain.

" Below there: Ho! " came a voice from the tree-top.

" Above there: Ho! " cried the captain.

" There is a cloud of dust on our direct front."

" Report again in two minutes," the captain called.

He slightly swung his sword belt, and half heaved his shield around.

" Stand to your arms! " he cried.

" Below there: Ho! " came the voice.

" Above: Ho! " cried the captain.

" There is a troop of horse on our direct front."

The captain became a meticulous energy.

" You," he cried, pointing, " to horse at

once.   Ride for your life to the palace.   Tell
each troop as you pass that the horses are
sighted.   The word is ' Mass on the western
outpost.'   Deliver that message at the palace.
Change horses there, and gallop back to me
to report that the message is delivered, and
that each troop on your route is massing to
fall in at our tail."

" You two," and he pointed again, one to
the right, one to the left, " warn all troops in
the round to muster on us."

He leaped on his horse, he galloped
around his squad to see that each mantle
was adjusted, each helmet burnished, each
arm in rigid order.

" We are the escort," he said.

And his teeth chattered as he spoke.

CHAPTER XLVII

WITHIN the palace there was a huge animation, and as colossal a silence.   The animation came from the multitude of those who
arrived with reports, and who departed with
instructions.

The silence came from the King.

It petrified his court, his officers, his guard. From daybreak he had sat in the Council Chamber, and men looked on a King they had never seen before.

Upright and silent and composed, he sat as a monster of granite might sit, and those stony jaws but opened to grind an enquiry and an order.

" Majesty! we are out ten miles in every direction."

" Move out twenty."

The officer returned.

" The roads are not clear to that distance, Lord! "

" Move out fifteen miles, and, as the roads clear, move again."

" It is a wide spacing and a great dispersal of the King's force."

" Let there be runners between all sections to warn of the massing point. Let the outward movement be slow, so that the horses may be fresh, and the return be at instant speed."

" We are drawing on the reserves, Majesty! "

" Draw to the limit."

" We are drawing on the palace guards, Majesty! "

" Leave but fifty."

" There are no more troops to draw on, Majesty! "

" You need move outwards no farther."

" Not even a fly could approach Tara undetected, Majesty! "

" Send urgent orders down each spoke of our great wheel that the centre of every space shall be left free for the returning messenger."

" Everything is ready, Majesty! "

" Let no trumpet be sounded except in that section which tells of the coming of the messenger.   When the trumpet is heard, let an hundred of the nearest troops be taken from another section and marched into the Hall of Ceremonies.   The King's Champion shall be in command of them. . . . The Herald! "

" Majesty! "

" Everything is in order, Herald? "

" Everything, Majesty! "

" The Queen knows the ceremony."

" She does, Majesty! "

" Recite the ceremony."

" When this gentleman is announced at

the walls the Queen will enter with her ladies.
The King and the Queen will take their seats.
Her ladies will stand behind the Queen: his
lords will stand behind the King: thirty men
at arms will form a circle about them and
about the stranger when he comes; seventy
soldiers in full harness will advance from the
walls and form a corridor from the armed
circle to the doorway.   When the gentleman
is introduced he will be ushered through that
corridor into that circle."

" Thus! "

" Majesty! "

" Speak."

" How shall this gentleman be introduced? "

" Let him be introduced as the Champion
Chess-Player of Ireland."

" If he has companions, Majesty? "

"He will have none but horse-boys.   I can
see him coming, Herald.   He will have
twenty horses, and ten horse-boys: each
riding a horse and leading a horse.   He will
ride in their front."

" Majesty! "

" Speak."

" What shall be done with those horses? "

" They shall be sent to the King's stables, and the horse-boys dismissed to their homes. . . . Herald! they shall be tracked to their homes by experienced men. You may go. Send me the Champion. . . . Herald! "

" Majesty? "

" This gentleman will bring with him a present of dogs for the King. That present will not be accepted. The dogs shall go back with the horse-boys. Send me the Champion."

CHAPTER XLVIII

THE Champion came, clanging in his battle-coats.

" Majesty! " he said.

" You know whom we expect, Champion?"

" The Chess-Player, Majesty."

" You are in command of the troops that will receive him."

The Champion's breast heaved and his carven face took on yet a writhe of grimness.

" The King honours me."

But Eochaid lifted blazing eyes to him—

" If that man should escape you——"

" I should be dead, Majesty."

" He could beat you, Champion."

" He could, Lord. He cannot beat me and an hundred men."

" I do not think he can. All must be done in order, Champion. The King will raise no hand against this person. He shall not be slain under the King's roof."

" He will be slain elsewhere, Lord."

" If he disavows his wager he shall go free, and the man that even breathes a violence against him shall die."

The Champion smiled:

" I shall seek him out another day, Majesty. I have a private matter with him."

" He will kill you, my friend."

" He smote me yesterday, in the King's presence. Already, since that smiting, I have lived too long."

" Champion! "

" Majesty? "

" Do you think that man will come? "

" As surely as the dawn has come, Majesty, that man will come."

" Will he abate his wager? "

" He will abate nothing."

" You feel that you are close to death, Champion! You feel that you know all things! "

" There is that which we think, master, and there is that which we know: the last is truth."

" You shall drink with me, Champion. Ho, there! A drink for the King and the King's Champion! "

The wine was brought.

" Drink me that measure, Champion: we may drink together again."

" You do not drink with me, Majesty! "

" Until this is finished I do not eat or drink. You shall drink the second goblet for me, and I shall kiss the brim of it. Sit by me."

" Champion! "
" Master? "
" What upholds that man? "
" The light in his head, master."
" And what is it that upholds the King? "
" The same light, master."

" Majesty! "
" What is it, Champion? "

" I am perhaps a little, a very little drunk! "

" That head and two measures of wine! No, Champion. It is the second sight that dazzles you."

" Dare I ask the King a question? "

" Ask it, friend! "

" Is the King even a little afraid of this Chess-Player? "

Eochaid turned his broad front to the Champion.

" By my hand! there not the weight of a fly's wing of fear within me. I have fronted this man as you have not: I have studied him as you have not. I feel in my hand and in my mind no loss of power. He has frightened you! "

" He has, Majesty."

" He has only made me wonder."

" The King has mustered an army to receive him! "

" And what of that? "

The Champion smiled apologetically.

" The Chess-Player has frightened me, but the King has made me wonder."

" It is common prudence," said Eochaid.

" The reserves used to the last man! The very palace guards depleted——! "

294

Eochaid's mouth came half open, and he stared at the Champion.

But it was within himself that he was staring.

" By my hand——! " he began.

There was heard a faint, clear call from far away; and in a moment a sharper note, and in ten seconds a trumpet blared at the walls—

The Champion did not bid the King adieu. He clanged from the table, from the room, to his post; and a violent messenger came flying to the King.

CHAPTER XLIX

THE stranger came, marching through that corridor of spears.

The purple mantle billowed behind him, showing, beneath, a tunic of golden thread. His ruddy-golden hair was caught at the sides in two shells of thin, pale, gold, and, from these, the diadem of a lesser king ran across his brow.

He strode into the great circle that
gleamed with helm and shield and shoulder-
plate, and a little smile of derision played
on his lips.

He bent to the High King, and he bowed
a full knee before the Queen.

" You are welcome to my Court," said
Eochaid.

" By my soul! Majesty, I have never
been received so royally. My escort was
fifteen miles long! "

" It should have been longer, but the
roads were not sufficiently clear. Audience
is granted to you, and you may speak."

" I have come through a land that bristles
in war! I am given audience in an armed
camp! I am vilely treated! "

" Yesterday, Chess Champion, when it
was dangerous to do so, you came armed
before the King; to-day you come unarmed,
and to-day is yet more dangerous."

" I have brought the King the horses
that he won, that stake is paid. I have
brought the King a present of forty great
dogs. I have paid my wager and my gift,
Majesty."

296

" That present will not be accepted, Chess Champion."

" The King's stake has not yet been paid! "

" Name your stake."

The stranger drew upright—

" I demand——"

" One moment, Chess Champion! The High King is generous. All this land and its fortunes are his. You may demand, even extravagantly. Name wisely your stake! "

The stranger brooded, almost gently, on the High King.

" What I ask I must ask, Majesty! "

Eochaid closed his eyes:

" Name your stake, Chess Champion! "

" I demand that the Queen, Etain, the King's wife, be given to me to be my wife.

No sound was heard in the vast room.

Not a piece of harness rattled, not a spear scraped on the floor.

To every person it seemed that for an eternal instant his heart had ceased to beat, and that he existed in a condition of time-less, motionless, dream.

Eochaid opened his eyes from a tranced

297

world.   Almost with amazement, he saw
that the stranger was still before him.   And
he saw that three hundred silent eyes had
moved from that grim person and were
staring silently upon himself.

CHAPTER L

No eye was resting on him in pity—the
moment was too tense.   No eye was looking
on him in sympathy—the curiosity was too
violent.

He was not looked upon as the King's
Majesty.

He was not seen as a human being.

He was brooded on with the passionate
detachment that is only given to an action.
He was the next move in a game, or a battle;
and, but for the staunchness of his soul, he
could have been whelmed in that inhuman
anonymity.

Indeed, his soul was stricken; and to get
to his feet he must lean both hands upon the
rests of his throne, and heave, so, upright.

The words that came from his lips were

blanched and toneless, and his eyes had grown so shy that they would not look at the stranger.

"Chess Champion," he said, "your stake is here. Take it."

"Lord," said the stranger, "my stake must be paid to me, must be given to me; as I have brought and paid and given."

And at that a pang of revolt massed Eochaid's body with blood and fire. . . .

An instant. . . .

It could not unfreeze his mind. It could not release him from the gluttonous eyes that flashed to the stranger, and that, with what abominable lack of sound, had spun, like active, indescribable beasts, like intelligent lightnings, back again to him, the King.

Were those eyes devouring him! Did they not actually taste his brawn and his blood!

Nay, they wanted none of his meat. They were stretching, thin-necked vampires, into his mind, to sip at the fountain of his pride; to drain his manhood!

Already he was dry as a tinder.

299

He was an empty husk.

The love of man had deserted him—that lovely loyalty was gone. The love of God was withdrawn—there was no responsibility—

A shield clanged on the floor, and a distraught being came running.

He was on his knees before the King, babbling, weeping, kissing the royal hands like a madman—

"Majesty—it is my right! He insulted me! I shall die of shame! It is my right . . .!"

Eochaid looked down on his hands and on the distorted face that adored him; and, as at a touch, he was released from every demon. His heart spoke, though his lips did not—

Dearest of my realm! said his heart. Comrade and friend and brother——!

"Single combat!" said the kneeler. "Here, in the presence of Ireland——!"

The King's great hands lifted the Champion.

"You shall fight no more," he said. "You shall stand always by the Throne."

He eyed the stranger:
" I shall pay my stake, and woe upon you,
horrible man ! "

CHAPTER LI

HE strode to the Queen, and took her
hand.

Her face dazzled and confounded him,
for it was white as snow, and the eyes that
he looked into were vast, and were pools of
terror.

He led her to the stranger.

" Chess Champion," he said, " here is
your stake."

" You pay me this stake? "

" I pay it."

" You give me the Queen, Etain, to be my
wife."

" I give her to you."

Each upon the other directed a look of
irrevocable hate.

" I wish to be alone with my wife," said
the stranger.

Eochaid returned to his throne.

" I wish this room to be cleared of all people," said the stranger.

" That will not be done," said Eochaid. " I have paid my stake. You have received it. You must now take it away—if you can."

A metallic whisper went through the great room as the soldiers present stiffened in their harness. The mind of every man of them fled sickeningly to his own boots, and the eye of every man looked horribly at the boots of his neighbour; and then, and again, they stared upon the stranger.

He brooded on the Queen: he bent a little to her.

" Etain! " he whispered.

Her hand flew to her forehead, where memory stirred like a dream.

" You do not remember me, Etain! You do not remember your true husband? "

She clasped, she wrung her hands:

" I do not remember you, sir."

" You will come with me."

" I will not go," said Etain.

And, as she spoke, she raised her head,

302

and, as a wild fawn lifts its crest and hearkens with all its members and with all its blood, so she listened:

"You hear?" said the stranger.

"The Bells!" said Etain. "So delicate! So sweet!"

"They soothe," he said, "they heal."

"The Bells have ceased," said Etain.

". . . There the primrose blows and blossoms in the hair. Snow-white are the arms of the maidens there. Strong are the men, and wise and fair, in the Wonderful Land.

"Will you, can you still delay? Grey and gloom are gone to-day. The world is gone, away, away, to the Wonderful Land . . ."

Her eyes were closed.

Her body swayed to the right, to the left. She should have fallen, but a strong arm was about her waist, and her head was lying on the breast of Midir.

As he touched her a harsh sob came from the onlookers: a gulp of rage and hatred.

A man dashed forward; and, on the instant, twenty men leaped, roaring:

303

But, even as they moved, they stopped. For, with the rapidity of light, Midir and Etain rose into the air; they floated through the roof; they disappeared.

The soldiers without knew nothing of that happening. But they told afterwards that they had seen the Flight of the Swans; two Snow-White Swans, linked by a silver chain; beating wide wings away to the West; beating away to Hy Brasil and the Lands of Faery.

THE END

Thus far the stories of Nera and of Etain, of Hy Brasil and the Lands of Faery, and of the Introduction to the Great Táin.

Printed in Great Britain by R. & R. CLARK, LIMITED, *Edinburgh.*